Betsy stood at the window and watched the wounded detective make his way across the beach. "Winnie, what do you think of the idea of Amanda and our young detective?" Betsy mused.

"As what?"

"As a couple, silly."

Winnie rolled her eyes and folded the paper. "Now, Betsy—"she began as she pulled off her glasses.

Betsy turned to make her case. "Well, why not? They have a great deal in common. They are both in pain—Amanda may be a bit further along the path from hers, but she understands pain in a way that no one else possibly could. Perhaps God sent Peter here so that he and Amanda might—"

"Your nephew sent him, dear."

Betsy laughed with delight. "Oh, Winnie, have you never heard that God works in mysterious ways?"

ANNA SCHMIDT

has been writing most of her life. Her first "critical" success was a short poem she wrote for a Bible study class in fourth grade. Several years later she launched her career as a published author with a two-act play and several works of nonfiction.

Anna is a transplanted Virginian, living now in Wisconsin. She works part-time doing public relations for an international company, and enjoys traveling, gardening, long walks in the city or country and antiquing. She is currently at work on a screenplay in addition to developing new story ideas for future novels.

LOVE NEXT DOOR

ANNA SCHMIDT

Steeple
Hill®

Published by Steeple Hill Books™

STEEPLE HILL BOOKS

Steeple Hill®

ISBN 0-373-87304-2

LOVE NEXT DOOR

www.SteepleHill.com

Printed in U.S.A.

Give a lad a training suitable to his character and,
even when old, he will not go back on it.
—*Proverbs* 22:6

For Jane

Chapter One

The door to the squad lounge slammed, shattering the quiet of the room like a single gunshot. Detective Pete Fleming steeled himself against the involuntary flinch, but he was a split second too late. His partner had noticed, just as he'd noticed the slight tremor in Pete's hand when he poured coffee.

"You could use some time," Jud Kalazinski muttered as he drained his coffee, smashed the cardboard cup into a quarter of its original size and tossed it across the room in the general direction of the overflowing trash can.

"I'm fine," Pete said, and demonstrated by refilling his coffee cup without the slightest hint of shakiness.

Jud turned his attention back to the sports page, but Pete knew the conversation wouldn't end there.

"You've got vacation coming. Take it."

"It's summer. We're busiest when they're out of school."

Jud gave a disbelieving hoot of laughter. "They don't go to school any season if they can get out of it. Who are you kidding?"

Myself, Pete thought, but said nothing.

Jud stood and stretched. "Take the time," he said, and just before he opened the door, added in a pretty good imitation of the captain's gruff tone, "That's an order, Detective Fleming."

Pete remained where he was, staring out the grime-covered window, observing the scene below, alert to any hint of trouble. That kid there at the corner, for instance. Pete quickly recorded the oversize jeans, the baggy sports jersey, the hat pulled low. He figured the kid was up to no good.

Suddenly the boy straightened and grinned at something he saw across the street. Tugging at his too-big jeans, he dodged traffic against the light and joined another boy. The two of them headed for the playground, bouncing a basketball between them as they walked.

Pete felt a blend of relief and disappointment. He wasn't often wrong. His instincts had always been his trademark—until recently. He released the blind and walked away as the slats clattered back into place.

Out in the squad room he walked the familiar path to his desk, which was positioned against the far wall. When he was in the squad room—which wasn't often—his back was to the others. He was a loner, but he was also the best, so no one took offense or complained. He headed for the desk, his head down, his stride as purposeful as possible given his limp.

In his peripheral vision, he caught the exchange of looks between the rookie and his partner. He saw the way Andrews suddenly found a need to bury himself in paperwork. He did not miss the rolled eyes and smirk of the transfer, DiMotto, who had positioned himself for a fight with Pete for top-cop status from day one.

Pete's desk was uncluttered, everything arranged in labeled files, all his supplies aligned precisely, not a single knot in his phone cord. He'd had some time these last few weeks. The note stood out, positioned as it was in the center of his desk. He recognized the captain's handwriting from ten feet away.

He snatched up the message and grabbed his jacket from the lopsided wooden coat rack near the back stairs. On his way out, he waved the paper in the general direction of the others, hoping they would all assume he had been handed an assignment.

He glanced at the message one more time when he hit the street, then crumpled the paper and tossed it into the nearest wastebasket.

Connie's Café. We need to talk.

Amanda Hunter pulled up the hood of her sweatshirt against the downpour as she ran from the office and infirmary across the campgrounds to the mess hall. By the time she reached the shelter of the oversize porch, she was soaked. Amanda pulled her clipboard from underneath her sweatshirt and smoothed out the top page. She stared at the list looking for any chore that she could accomplish in the pouring rain.

The aging buildings of the camp were always a challenge to get into shape for the season. No matter how hard she worked at keeping them updated and well-maintained, she always seemed to be playing catch-up. This year she was further behind than ever. It was time to admit that she might not be able to keep doing this on her own.

In just two days, this year's group of college-age counselors and high-school-age junior counselors would arrive for orientation and a week of bonding before the campers came. For the most part everything was ready, except for getting the pier into the lake and bringing the canoes and small sailboats out of storage and down to the edge of the sand beach. Oh, and raking that same sand beach and repairing the winter damage to the lifeguard stand and—the list went on for three pages and there was little she could do until the rain let up. At least the cabins were ready.

Amanda plopped down onto one of the long wooden benches that lined the porch and flipped open her cell phone. Three messages, all from Dan Roark, the local handyman and owner of his own construction company. Dan had been helping her out ever since…ever since…

She paused and stared out at the gray choppy water. After two years, it was still impossible to put words to the loss of her husband and son. Somewhere out there on a beautiful summer's night, they had struggled and drowned. She swallowed the lump that came automatically every time she remembered.

"Focus," she muttered and turned her attention back to the phone. She listened to the messages. Dan was tied up. The rains had been especially steady all spring and his business in construction depended on the cooperation of the weather.

"I'll try to make it before the counselors get here, but you might just have to make the pier their first project, Mandy." His words crackled as the connection from cell to cell struggled to stay intact.

Amanda pocketed the phone. Nope. The pier was always in when the counselors arrived. As they got off the bus, they saw the camp welcoming and waiting for them, filled with possibilities. It had been that way every summer since Amanda's grandparents had first opened the place back in the fifties. She had never missed having everything ready. Even the year after the accident, her friends and neighbors had made sure everything was done. To her way of thinking, there was simply no excuse for not having it done this year, as well.

She leaned back against the thick log wall of the large building that served as both dining and assembly hall, propping her feet on the porch railing to watch the rain. The sound of the steady downpour was comforting and restful. She closed her eyes and let the rhythm of it surround her. Peace. Serenity. Consolation.

Was God sitting up there in that sky filled with rolling gray clouds, looking down on her with a satisfied smile? *Made you stop and smell the raindrops, didn't I?* she imagined Him saying. She closed her eyes and gave herself up to the rare moment of peace and quiet. She could count on not having such a moment again for at least six weeks.

She recalled her grandfather telling her that just when people thought they had the world by the tail and were in total control—as she had these last few days—God sent something to remind them otherwise. Sometimes it was subtle, like a rain shower. Other times it was like a punch in the face when you least expected it. Or maybe Gramps had that wrong—maybe sometimes it wasn't God at all, but some darker force.

Amanda opened her eyes, but she didn't move. She

stared at the lake—at the agitated churning and threatening water that would calm with the passing of the storm, turn a beautiful blue and sparkle invitingly. Her thoughts always came back to that terrible night—the night that had changed her life forever.

Connie's Café was a hole-in-the-wall place by the river. It was dark and smelled of stale beer and decades of cigar smoke, and it was the captain's preferred venue for talking privately. Pete had taken a circuitous route, in case DiMotto or any of the others were watching from the window. As a result, it took him twenty minutes to reach the place instead of the usual five.

Inside, he blinked to get his eyes used to the change in light, nodded to Conrad Hess, the owner and sole employee, then headed straight for the corner table in the back of the otherwise deserted place.

"Sit," Captain Bingle said without looking up. He was scribbling numbers on a piece of paper.

Pete sat. Connie approached but the captain waved him away. Then to Pete's surprise, Bingle put his pen back in his pocket, leaned back in his chair and smiled.

"How's that book of yours coming along?" he asked affably.

Pete was confused and confusion always triggered caution for him. "It's Andrews who's writing the book."

"Maybe you ought to give it a shot."

The captain continued to observe Pete. He was smiling pleasantly as if they were discussing yesterday's sports news, but his eyes were intense and unwavering. Pete could almost feel the heat of the older man's gaze. He knew that even in the dim light of the café, there was no hiding the heavy bags from not enough sleep, the lines etched deeper than ever in his forehead, the sallow cast to his usually tan skin. He shifted to put himself deeper into shadow.

"I'm not much of a writer, Captain."

Bingle pounced on that. The chair slammed forward on all fours and suddenly his face was not four inches from Pete's nose. "You're not much of a detective right now, son."

Pete went on instant defense. No excuses, just whatever it took to fight for his job. "I'm working it out."

The captain slid the paper across the table. "Go work on it away from here. This is my aunt's name and number. She's expecting your call. She has a place up on Lake Geneva. There's a furnished boathouse. I'll see you in six weeks."

The captain stood up, threw some bills on the table and headed for the door. "Get him a sandwich, Con. He's going undercover and it'll be a while before he can taste that barbecued chicken of yours."

Pete heard the door close, heard Con preparing the food. He knew what the captain had just done for him. Telling Con he was putting Pete undercover assured that that news would spread to others on the force. The captain was giving him a way to take the time he needed without sacrificing his macho. Bingle was a class act. He also expected to be obeyed without question. He'd given Pete a direct order—there was no possibility of turning it down.

Pete picked up the paper the captain had left on the table, pushed back his chair and went down the narrow hall to the alley outside the back exit. He flipped open his cell phone and punched in the numbers from the scrap of paper.

It was hard to miss the huge Bingle estate. Lake Geneva, Wisconsin, was a far cry from the south side of Chicago. A massive stone house with dozens of small-paned windows sat high on the hill. The drive from the road wound half a mile through woods. On the other side of the house, lush green grass that would have been the envy of any golf course cascaded down to the water's edge. Gardens to either side of the mansion were a riot of late-spring color. Pete stood on the expansive enclosed porch and stared out at the lake, trying hard to reconcile the paradox of staring out the grimy window of the squad room a day earlier and standing now in what seemed as unreal as a movie set.

"It's early in the season," Betsy Bingle said as she emerged from the house followed by Winnie Cromwell. From what Pete could gather, Winnie was like the faithful companion of days gone by. She carried a large silver tray loaded with a flowered china teapot and matching cups and saucers that looked more vulnerable than the paper cups Jud routinely crushed after coffee in the break room. There were also two plates—one with tiny little sandwiches that would barely qualify as bite-size, and the other a tiered-glass thing filled with some pretty good-looking chocolate brownies and cookies.

"Whenever weather permits we always take tea out here at four," the old lady said, indicating that Pete should sit in one of the half-dozen wicker rocking chairs positioned to take in the view and permit conversation.

"It's loosely referred to as a three-season room. However, the person who coined that term clearly never lived in Wisconsin. Lemon, Detective?"

Pete shook his head. The setting was surreal to say the least. Him taking tea with two elderly women for one thing. Ever alert, he inventoried the sounds—the clink of silver on china, a single small motorboat down on the lake, and birds—lots of birds. He was accustomed to city noises, and this much peace and quiet was downright unnerving.

"Rudy—your Captain Bingle—" she added with a smile, "always loved the lump sugar. He'd put half a dozen in the cup before allowing me to pour. It's a wonder the boy has an original tooth in his head with all that sugar."

Pete declined the sugar she held before him with a pair of tiny silver tongs. He concentrated on not breaking off the delicate cup handle and settled for holding the bottom of the teacup in the palm of his hand.

"This is very kind of you, Ms. Bingle," he began when there was no further conversation.

"Oh, Detective, make it Betsy, please. It's *Miss* Bingle and I do tire of explaining my single state. I mean, surely a woman approaching eighty-five should not have to explain why she chose not to marry."

His detective's curiosity got the better of him. "And why *did* you choose not to marry?" he asked.

She beamed. "Oh, I do like you immensely already, Detective. So direct and inquisitive. Isn't he quite marvelous, Winnie?"

Pete actually felt heat rising to his cheeks and was surprised that the sensation was a pleasant one. "It's just Pete, ma'am," he said, "and you can ignore my curiosity if it's out of line. Asking questions comes with the job."

"Oh, no," she exclaimed. "It's high time we had some interesting conversation around here. Poor Winnie and I have said just about everything there could possibly be to say over the last thirty or so years. Now, what was the question?"

"The detective asks why you chose not to marry," Winnie reminded her with a smile.

"Because I never found a man who could hold a candle to friends like this dear lady when it came to intelligent conversation." She patted Winnie's hand and it was Winnie's turn to blush.

Pete relaxed slightly and reached for another sandwich. "And you felt the same way, Ms. Cromwell—about men, I mean?"

Winnie hooted with laughter and delight and Pete found himself chuckling, something he also hadn't done in a while.

"No, no Detective—Pete! I was married. To a man fifteen years my junior. Who would think I would be the one to outlive him?"

"Yes," Betsy interrupted. "Winnie was quite the talk of the town when she had the audacity to accept a proposal from a man so much younger than she. That disparity in age seems to work fine for men and their little trophy wives, but women are supposed to have more dignity than to indulge in such silliness."

Winnie smiled at her and continued. "When Edgar died, I was frankly adrift."

Betsy rushed to complete the story. "Then I said,

'Well come here and stay with me.' And that was that."
She refilled their teacups and as she set the teapot on the
ornate tray, added, "And what of you, Pete? You must
be what—forty?"

"Thirty-two," Pete replied. He stroked his clean-
shaven chin and brushed his hair away from his forehead. He must look worse than he thought.

"Ah, well, Rudy did say you'd had a bit of a rough
go lately. The fresh air and quiet here will have you
looking younger in no time." She blinked rapidly several times and turned to Winnie.

"You wanted to ask the detective why he has never
married," Winnie prompted.

"Indeed I did," Betsy said with a beaming smile.
"Well?"

"I never found a woman who interested me enough,"
he replied with a grin. "Not until now at least."

Betsy paused and studied him closely, the same way
the captain had back at the café. "You have such a lovely
smile. You must learn to use it with abandon." She
touched his cheek and Pete was stunned to feel a lump
in his throat.

He stood and cleared his throat as he looked out to
the lake and regained his composure. "Your place is
certainly impressive, ma'am."

He heard her sigh. "Now, Pete, it is to be Betsy and
Winnie. If you insist on treating us like old fogies, we
shall never have any fun at all."

"Yes, ma'am," Pete said, and then caught himself.
"I'll do my best, Betsy. Thank you for letting me come."

Betsy waved away his gratitude with an impatient
fling of her long fingers. "Take this charmer down to the

boathouse, Winnie," she said, "and see that he's settled in. Supper is at seven," she added, "and you may join us or not but we do dress for dinner, Detective. It's the absence of the proper civilities that has wrecked society, if you ask me."

"Yes, ma'am."

He followed Winnie down the curved stone stairway and across the lawn to the boathouse.

"Thank you for coming here, Detective," Winnie said as she unlocked the door to the living space above the actual boat storage. "She's been failing lately and Rudy's call brightened her considerably. Then, when you called, she was absolutely her old self again, filled with plans. You may as well settle in and let her make a fuss over you."

Pete hesitated before answering. It had been a pleasant hour, but he wasn't in the mood for a steady diet of tea and crumpets. "I'm not sure what the captain told you...."

"Everything," Winnie replied soberly. "Don't worry, Betsy and I both understand why you've come and your need for peace and solitude. Just know that we're up there and the invitation stands. You'd be doing her a kindness to take her up on the invitation for tea or supper once in a while. Khakis and a sport jacket are fine as proper dinner dress."

"Good. I'm afraid I left my tux back in Chicago."

"Well, this is it and I do mean this is the whole of it," Winnie said, taking in the large open space with a sweep of one hand. "Bathroom through there. Sleeping loft up there. Plenty of storage and books—more books in the library up at the house if you don't find anything to your taste here." She moved around opening cabinets to display their contents and demonstrating the ceiling fan. "Not a lot of need for air-conditioning, but you have the window unit in the loft just in case. Wood for the fireplace is kept along the wall below next to the pontoon. There's a canoe down there, as well. Feel free to make use of whatever is here."

"What's next door?" Pete had wandered over to the patio door.

"Over there is the Hancock place. New money from Chicago. They tore down a treasure and put up that monstrosity," Winnie sniffed. "Blessedly, they only use it about one weekend out of the season, so Betsy and I ignore it most of the time."

"And over there?" Pete indicated the other side.

Winnie crossed to the windows on the other side and motioned toward the property beyond the wild gardens. "Ah. Camp Good News. It's been in the same family for more than half a century. The granddaughter has it now—Amanda. She's quite amazing. She…"

"A camp—like a campground with RVs and such?"

Winnie laughed. "Oh, my, no, dear boy. A camp for young boys. Troubled city youths in need of a second chance. Amanda and her family have changed more than one young life for the better. Six weeks at Camp Good News can sometimes make all the difference."

Pete frowned. The last thing he needed was a bunch of young toughs living next door. What was the captain thinking?

"Rudy attended the camp in his youth," Winnie continued as she moved around the small apartment, checking to be sure there were towels, rearranging the vase of fresh flowers and adding fruit from the small refrigerator to the fruit bowl on the kitchen counter. "Betsy demanded that he come every summer and become a counselor when he was old enough. He was quite a handful in his youth. His parents were absolutely beside themselves. Then Betsy brought him here." Winnie paused in the action of fluffing a throw pillow on the sofa and smiled at the memory. "Poor lad, he saw the grand estate and thought he was home free. Then Betsy marched him next door. The look on that boy's face!"

She handed Pete the key. "Well, I'll let you settle in. Don't hesitate to call if you need anything. Just press that button there. It's the intercom between here and the main house."

"Thanks. I mean it, thanks a lot. It's nice and I haven't taken time in a while to…"

Winnie grasped Pete's hand in both of hers. "Oh, my dear boy, after what you've been through, we are so glad to be able to help." Pete was afraid the older woman might actually hug him. But instead, Winnie turned and fled from the room.

By the time Pete had unpacked, showered and changed into shorts and a T-shirt, it was after six. He stretched out on the chaise lounge on the lawn next to the boathouse to enjoy the sunset. A woman was down at the neighboring beach. She was tall and slim and wearing denim cutoffs and a sweatshirt about three sizes too large for her.

Probably her husband's shirt, Pete thought as he gingerly stretched out the leg where he'd taken the bullet. He allowed himself to observe the woman, knowing that she was unaware that she was being watched. She wrestled with a short section of a pier that had been stored on shore over the winter, tugging and pulling it until it was positioned at the water's edge. He saw her look back at the remaining sections and her shoulders drooped. Then she straightened and pulled her work gloves more securely into place as she headed back across the sand to tackle the next section. Apparently it was her plan to line the pieces up on land before getting them into the water.

Pete considered walking over to offer a hand, but he'd come here to be alone, and if he helped the woman, no doubt she'd want to repay him in some way. Where was her husband?

He surveyed the neighboring property. Through the overgrown border of Betsy Bingle's gardens, he couldn't see much. A cluster of small cabins and a larger log structure. A flag pole. Please tell me they don't do reveille at sunrise, he thought. The one thing he knew for certain was that the camp was a far cry from the Bingle estate. An oddity on a lake where nineteenth-century captains of industry had built their massive summer cottages, and their twentieth-century counterparts had torn them down and built their own castles to success.

"Amanda Hunter! Stop that right this instant!" Betsy Bingle's voice rang out from above. The woman on the beach dropped the dock section and shielded her eyes as she looked up toward Betsy's veranda. Then she grinned and waved. Obviously, from her vantage point high on the hill, Betsy Bingle could keep her eye on everything going on around her.

"It's got to get done," the woman on the beach shouted cheerfully.

"Well, not by you alone and not tonight. Where's Dan?"

"He's backed up with other work."

"Then you'll make it a project for the children when they arrive tomorrow. The physical labor will do them good."

The woman laughed and pulled off her gloves, dropping them on the dock section as she climbed the slope and disappeared behind the barrier of overgrown vegetation that blocked Pete's view.

"Aye, aye, Captain," Pete heard her call as she reappeared through a break in the shrubbery.

"Really, Ensign Hunter, you know that I prefer to be addressed as Admiral," Betsy replied. Their laughter drifted through the dusk as they each returned to their respective houses. Obviously an inside joke between the two women. Even though Pete didn't understand the humor, it was nice to see neighbors acting civilly— even warmly—to each other. Too often on his beat they were at each other's throats.

Amanda Hunter. Pete had no idea why he'd recorded her name—nice name but of absolutely no possible use to him. Force of habit. He leaned back in the chaise and promptly fell asleep.

After supper, Amanda put the finishing touches on the schedule and cabin assignments. The basic schedule hadn't changed much in years. Wake-up and cabin check followed by breakfast. She chuckled as she recalled how excited the head cook, Edna Watson, had been when Amanda told her that she wanted the menus to focus on healthy and diverse foods for the summer.

"They'll turn up their noses and refuse to touch the stuff," Edna had warned.

"They'll come around if they get hungry enough," Amanda had replied, and that had been all Edna needed. So far she had already called three times during the week to discuss her ideas for ethnic menus.

Amanda turned her attention back to the schedule. After breakfast came clean-up, which included cabins, laundry, kitchen duty and anything else that might arise. She filled in the chart with cabin numbers for each chore on a rotating basis.

The rest of the day was taken up with a variety of activities—swimming, wilderness training, crafts, music, canoeing, team sports. The goal was to keep the campers so busy that they had no time to get into trouble and were relieved to have the chance to play cards or board games or read in the evenings until lights out. Each day ended with vespers at sunset, on the beach if weather permitted or in the dining hall if not.

Amanda leaned back and stared at the names of this summer's campers. She could barely keep her eyes open, and she rejoiced in her exhaustion. A good night's sleep was exactly what she needed to be ready for another successful camp season. The last two seasons had gone by in a blur. The first year after the accident, she had had no heart or stomach for the task. It was Betsy Bingle who had urged her forward.

"One step at a time," Betsy had counseled. "One minute, one hour, one day and then another until you've made it through the year. It has to be done, Amanda."

Amanda had known that Betsy was right. There was no way to find her way out of the tunnel of her grief except by forcing herself forward through the hours and days and the long lonely nights of her mourning.

She barely remembered anything of that first summer. In the winter that followed she had traveled—first to Europe and then from college campus to college campus recruiting staff and counselors for the next season. She and Stan had always done that together until Danny was in school.

This last winter and spring she'd mostly stayed home, living in the house she'd grown up in and had lived in after her marriage. She had finally been ready to deal with all the memories and put them in their proper place. Memories were, by definition, a segment of the past. Living was for the present, and dreams and hopes were the stuff of the future, according to Betsy. Betsy was a firm believer in the principle of carpe diem.

"Well, Boo, if we're to 'seize the day' tomorrow, we'd better get some sleep. Come on, go outside."

The soft-coated wheaten terrier that she and Stan had gotten for Danny the year of the accident trotted out to the front porch. He stretched and then squeezed through the doggie door Stan had installed in the screen. Amanda smiled as with an effort, the dog pulled his expanding hips through the small hole. "We're going to cut back on those treats, Boo," she said. "It's time you started eating better, too." Boo ignored her as he trotted down the hill toward the boathouse.

"Just mind your own business, Boo," she called, but then she smiled and stood there watching him disappear through the heavy shrubs that separated the Bingle property from hers. She knew where he was headed. She had kept him inside from the time she'd seen Betsy's houseguest moving into the boathouse. Boo couldn't wait to get down there and check things out for himself. He was as curious about their new neighbor as Amanda was.

Chapter Two

Okay, so now he was dreaming about her. He hadn't even gotten a good look at her. She could be fifty. She could kiss though. He'd give her that, although he might have to find a way to speak to her about that fuzz on her face and her breath was not quite as fresh as...

Pete came fully awake without moving a muscle. It was pitch black and someone—*something* was lying on his chest. Twenty-five...maybe thirty pounds. Could be a small bear. Out here in the wilds, there must be bears. He glanced around, his eyes growing accustomed to the dark. The furry thing was white. *A polar bear?*

"Boo?" This was followed by a low whistle.

The call came from the woman next door whose name had just flown out of his mind in the face of his current situation. The thing on his chest gave a low growl.

"Boo, come on. I know you're out there. We've got a big day tomorrow." Another whistle—through her teeth like a man might whistle approval at a sports event or rock concert.

Impressive.

The thing on his chest dug in its claws and stretched, then dropped nimbly to the ground and trotted down the deck steps and around the side of the boathouse. A moment later, Pete heard "Good dog. That's my good boy." A screen door slammed.

Pete let out a breath. A dog. He started to chuckle, then he was laughing and he couldn't seem to stop. Big bad Detective Pete Fleming had been paralyzed with fear by a little white dog named Boo.

Maybe the captain and Jud were right. Maybe he did need some time. If he could lose it over a stupid dog, he must be in more trouble than he'd allowed himself to admit.

Who would name a dog Boo?

Amanda Hunter. Her name came back to him, and he felt better than he had in weeks. Wide awake now, he noticed the sections of the pier still lined up on the beach. Apparently, her husband hadn't gotten around to finishing it. He decided to head down to the beach and see what he could do about getting the rest of the pier set up for her.

Amanda knew there was little point in arguing with Dan Roark once he'd set his mind on something.

"I'm on my way," he announced.

"It's late," she protested. "I can have the counselors do it tomorrow. Get some rest."

"I'll just stop by and check things out," he insisted. "Be sure you've got everything you need to put the thing in the water. I'm nearly there and it's on my way and…"

Amanda laughed. "All right," she said. "I give up. At least say you'll stay for coffee."

"Make it decaf and throw in a couple of your famous lemon bars and I'm all yours. See you in a few minutes."

Amanda added one last item to her list of things to do before the counselors arrived, then put on a fresh pot of coffee and walked out onto the screened porch wrapped protectively around the house to wait for Dan. Boo was usually back and curled up on the porch swing by this time. But tonight he'd obviously decided to do a thorough job of checking out Betsy's houseguest.

On her second call, she watched Boo race up the hill as if the devil himself were on his tail. He slid to a stop at the foot of the stairs to the porch and waited for Amanda to open the screen door for him. Then he trotted past her and into the house. He attacked his water bowl, filling the silence of the night with the sounds of his slurping and the scraping of the ceramic bowl against the wood floor as he pushed his nose into every crevice to get the last drops.

Amanda grinned and looked out toward the beach. Lights were on in the boathouse. She had questions of her own about the sudden appearance of the stranger. Betsy had been very evasive about telling her anything. And Winnie, who usually loved to be the bearer of news, had also been uncommonly silent.

Neither woman had mentioned any plans for a houseguest, especially one coming for an extended stay. One day when she'd seen Winnie cleaning the boathouse, Amanda had gone over to see what was going on. The boathouse hadn't been used in years. But the only thing she'd found out was that the man was a friend of Betsy's nephew, Rudy, and he would be recuperating there for a number of weeks.

She watched as Betsy's houseguest walked across the beach. Actually it was more like an attempt at striding, but his limping gait made that impossible. Betsy had also been vague about why he was here. Under questioning, it was obvious that she really didn't know him at all. And why the boathouse, since Betsy had plenty of room in the main house?

She studied the man as he moved along the shore. His shoulders sagged and his pace was uneven—a few steps and then a pause as he stared out over the lake. Then, head bent, he trudged on with that decided limp. Judging by all that, Amanda would have guessed him to be up in years, but she seemed to recall that Betsy kept referring to him as "our young friend." Of course to Betsy, most people were her "young" friends.

He stopped and looked at the last pieces of the pier that she had left for morning. He stooped to lift one and she was about to head down to the beach to stop him when she heard Dan's truck pull into the drive. Better to let him handle this. Since Rudy Bingle was with the police force in Chicago, the visitor could be someone he was protecting—perhaps a key witness or even a criminal who had decided to give evidence in return for a plea bargain. What better place to hide out than Betsy Bingle's boathouse?

Betsy stood at the window and watched the wounded detective make his way across the beach. Slowly, methodically, he moved the sections of the pier into place. At this rate it would take him hours, but perhaps that was what was needed. Hard physical labor to push out the memories, the questions and doubts.

"Winnie, dear?"

Winnie glanced up from the newspaper and peered over the rims of her reading glasses.

"I was thinking…" Betsy mused.

"That's usually a dangerous thing, Betsy."

"I'll ignore that." She continued watching Pete Fleming.

"And what were you thinking?" Winnie prompted.

"What do you think of the idea of Amanda and our young detective?"

"As what?"

"As a couple, silly."

Winnie rolled her eyes and folded the paper. "Now, Betsy—" she began as she pulled off her glasses.

Betsy waved an impatient hand at her and turned back to the window. "Well, why not? They have a great deal in common."

"You don't know that."

Betsy turned to make her case. "They are both in pain— Amanda may be a bit further along the path from hers, but she understands pain in a way that no one else possibly could. Perhaps God sent Pete here so that he and Amanda might—"

"Your nephew sent him, dear."

Betsy laughed with delight. "Oh, Winnie, have you never heard that God works in mysterious ways?"

"Who's that?"

Dan Roark stood on the porch with a mug of coffee in one hand and a half-eaten lemon bar in the other.

"He's staying in Betsy's boathouse for a few weeks."

"Did you ask him to put the pier in?" Dan sounded hurt.

"Of course not. I don't even know the man."

Dan set his coffee on the willow side table and dusted the powdered sugar off his hands. "Well, might as well give him a hand before he messes the job up altogether."

He pushed open the screen and was halfway down the path and across the camp compound before Amanda could stop him.

She watched as the two men introduced themselves and then started to work. She thought about going down and lending a hand herself, but they seemed to have everything organized and she knew that Dan really wanted to finish the pier for her.

Dan Roark had been Stan Hunter's best friend, as well as godfather to their son, Danny. She and Stan had named their son after him in tribute to that lifelong friendship. In the days following the accident, Dan had been a basket case and Amanda had found that consoling him had helped her through those first horrible days. Since then Dan had been her friend and protector. There was nothing romantic about their relationship. Dan was very much in love with his wife, Dottie, and he adored their three daughters. But he had seen it as his duty to Stan's memory to watch over Amanda.

Most of the time, it was touching, and Amanda could not deny that in those first months, she had found it very comforting. Every once in a while though, Dan tended to act a little too much like a big brother protecting his innocent little sister from the big bad world. She hoped he wasn't being too hard on Betsy's houseguest.

* * *

The man introduced himself as Dan Roark. They shook hands and then both took a moment to survey the project before them.

"You ever put a pier in before?" Dan asked.

"First time," Pete replied.

"Thought so," Dan said and there was no judgment in his tone. "I'll just get a few tools from the shed there." He walked a short distance across the sand beach while Pete continued to consider the pieces of the puzzle before him. The truth was he was very glad that Dan had shown up.

"She put some of it in by herself earlier," Pete reported when Dan returned.

"She thinks she's got super powers. I told her I'd get it done. She likes everything in place before the counselors get here. Take hold of that corner there, will you?"

For the next hour Pete followed instructions. It was clear that Dan knew exactly what he was doing, and there was little talk other than the exchange of directions. It was hard physical work and Pete relished the challenge. It struck him that he wasn't going to be much good at lying around for the next few weeks. Maybe there was something he could do for Betsy Bingle—clean out those gardens or something.

"Well, that's it," Dan announced as he waded back into shore after checking to be sure everything was perfect. "Couldn't have done it without you, Pete. Mandy'll be real pleased."

The two men shook hands again. "Glad I could do it," Pete said, and then there didn't seem to be anything more to do other than walk back across the beach to the boathouse.

Pete was a keen observer of others and there was something about Dan that just didn't seem to fit. Before the work had overshadowed further small talk, Pete had learned that Dan had his own construction business and picked up odd jobs when things were slow. That made sense as to why he hadn't been around earlier when the woman was lugging the pier around by herself.

The difference in last names didn't even faze him. After all, in the city half the married people he knew used different last names or hyphenated the two or some such nonsense. If he ever married, he hoped his wife would want to take his name. To his way of thinking they were starting a new family and he sure didn't want their kids having to explain why their married parents had two different names. Call me old-fashioned, but some traditions should be revered.

When he reached the boathouse, he looked back. Dan locked the shed after replacing the tools and headed back up toward the log house on the hill. In spite of his earlier reservations, Pete was impressed with the layout of the camp. Six cabins plus what he took to be a combination infirmary and administrative building lined one side of the compound. A large ancient log structure anchored the opposite side. In the woods beyond were three shelters furnished with picnic tables and stone barbecue pits. Overlooking everything was a modest but picturesque log house that glowed with light and was decidedly more welcoming than many of the places he'd passed on his drive to the Bingle estate.

"Seems like a decent sort," Dan announced when he returned to Amanda's house. "Not much of a talker though."

"It was really nice of him to want to help. I'll take over some baked goods tomorrow."

Dan grinned. "When? If I know you, you'll be up before sunrise and going eighty miles an hour well into the night."

Amanda walked with Dan out to his truck. "You worry too much," she said.

He climbed in and started the motor. "Anything else you need, you know the number. Dottie'll be here first thing. You girls have a good first day tomorrow."

Amanda waved and then returned to the house. She wrapped the rest of the lemon squares in foil and then pulled a package of chocolate chip cookies and another of brownies from the freezer. She arranged everything in a basket with a colorful dishtowel as the liner while Boo sat hopefully at her ankles watching every move.

"This is not for you, Mr. Boo, so just get those big eyes right back in your head." She set the basket on top of the refrigerator and turned out the kitchen light.

"Come on, Boo. Let's get some sleep. Big day tomorrow."

Used to the sounds of the city, Pete found sleep impossible. After getting the dock into place, he showered and got into bed and then just lay there, listening to the silence. The absence of identifiable chaos made him jumpy, so he got up, made himself a sandwich, popped a soda and went out onto the deck to eat. Within fifteen minutes the bugs had driven him back inside.

He flicked on the small television and checked out the six available channels—two home-shopping and four infomercials. He sprawled in the well-used recliner and concentrated on learning about the incredible advantages of working out on a piece of home exercise equipment that looked as though it would take Betsy Bingle's enormous dining room to house. The last thing he remembered was amusing himself by counting just how many times the announcer gave the toll-free number for ordering.

The dream came, as it always did, in pieces and out of sequence. Now a neighborhood gathering, laughter, music, good food, the smell of charcoal and sweat and hot dogs. Faces—some familiar, some not, some distorted into grotesque smiles. Too-loud voices speaking garbled words that Pete couldn't understand.

This signaled the turning point. The kid, on the fringes of the laughter and music and loud talk. The kid, shifty-eyed and sneaky, or could that have been panic and fear? The kid moving through the crowd, something in his hand. Not the perp he was after, but worth watching all the same. Then day was suddenly night and the clamor of the crowd was the chaos of a street mob, angry and panicked about something he couldn't understand.

Pete pushed his way forward, but it wasn't him. It was the captain pushing through the crowd while Pete stood there, his service revolver on the ground beside the kid, one round fired. The kid lying on the street, his face peaceful and undisturbed by the turmoil around him, his T-shirt soaked with blood, and in his open hand—a soda can.

Now the dream moved into slow motion. The shout behind him, the crowd parting. He could feel his own blood oozing down his leg, soaking his pants. He could feel the heat and pain of the open wound on his thigh.

He kept looking down at the can in the boy's hand. Pete had been shot, and he had fired back. His head reeled with the confusion of unanswered questions and impossible events that whirled around him. A mother's gut-wrenching wail and the echo of that single shot playing over and over in Pete's head.

He came instantly awake as he always did. Usually what woke him was the backfire of a car or the clatter of a garbage-can lid beneath his window at the precise moment of the shot in the dream. This time there was no car and no garbage can. Something else had awakened him. Daylight was streaming through the open door to the deck—the same door he was positive he had closed tightly the night before. Then he heard rustling in the kitchen. With practiced stealth he eased himself from the chair and reached for his service revolver on the top shelf of the floor-to-ceiling bookcases. The kid's family had promised revenge, even though Pete had been exonerated. In the past weeks there had been threatening letters and calls, slashed tires and a break-in at his apartment. Could they have followed him here?

He removed the safety and edged toward the kitchen. The rustling continued. Pete spun around so that he was standing in the open doorway to the kitchen, blocking any attempt at escape. He aimed his gun at the intruder. "Freeze!" he ordered.

The dog did as he was told for about half a second and then seeing Pete, he returned to his work. He was standing on top of the counter working his way through the loaf of bread Pete had left open after making his sandwich the night before. The soda can rolled across the floor where it had fallen in concert with the gunshot in his dream.

"How did you get in here?" Pete demanded and only then realized the ridiculousness of posing that question to a dog. More annoyed at himself than the dog, he brandished the gun in the general direction of the open door to the deck. "Go on. Get outta here."

The dog looked from Pete to the bread and back to Pete.

"Now!" He recalled the command the dog's owner had uttered the night before. It worked.

The dog made a grab for one more piece of bread, leaped down from the counter and tore through the living room and out the door. Once safely outside, he paused for a firmer hold on his booty, then strolled across the beach to where his mistress was wielding a sledgehammer almost bigger than she was as she drove a stake for a volleyball court into the soft sand.

"Where did you get that, Boo?" Pete heard her ask the dog. Then she turned around and leaned on the sledgehammer as she looked up at Pete.

"You really don't want to feed him," she called. "He has the world's greatest memory for those who give him treats and he'll drive you crazy."

Lady, he's already got a good start on that and… "I didn't feed him."

He watched her digest that, then turn on the dog. "Boo Hunter, you bad dog." She placed her free hand on her hip and the dog sat and stared up at her, still holding the bread clenched in his mouth.

"Well, what do you have to say for yourself?" she demanded.

Boo dropped the bread and lay down, placing his face between his front paws.

"Well, I should think so," the woman commented.

She turned back to Pete. "Sorry. It won't happen again," she called.

"It was my fault," Pete astonished himself by calling back. "I left the bread out." A comment which did nothing to address the fact that the little beggar had actually broken into the boathouse and made himself at home on the kitchen counter.

The woman was still staring at him and suddenly Pete was acutely aware that he was standing there in nothing but his pajama bottoms and holding a revolver in his right hand. "Later," he called and waved that same right hand, then dropped it to his side as he automatically checked again to make sure the safety was back in place and stepped back inside the boathouse.

"Thanks for helping Dan put in the pier," she yelled.

He waved—this time with his other hand—and shut the door, making sure it was completely closed.

It was a full minute before he heard the rhythmic pounding of the sledgehammer on the stake. The sight of the gun must have been a real shocker.

Okay, that did it. The man had a gun. Amanda gave the stake a final hit, dropped the hammer and marched straight up the hill to Betsy's.

"Betsy?"

"Come in, dear. We're just finishing breakfast, but I'm sure that—"

"Your houseguest has a gun."

"Well, of course, dear. He's a detective back in Chicago. They carry weapons."

"He's a policeman?"

"A detective, Amanda. I think they like the distinction," Winnie said in sotto voce as if someone might overhear her.

"A detective then. Why is he here?"

Betsy blinked. "Surely you have noticed that the poor man is wounded."

"He took one in the leg," Winnie added with a knowing nod.

"He has come here to recuperate," Betsy explained patiently. "I think that rest and a bit of physical activity will do wonders. I noticed he was helping Dan last night. That's a good sign, don't you think?"

"That does not explain why he was waving a gun at me this morning." An overstatement, but sometimes embellishment was called for in talking to Betsy.

Winnie and Betsy looked at each other. "Perhaps you should ask him," Winnie suggested.

Amanda was close to losing her patience with the two elderly women. "Are you telling me that you are not alarmed by this?"

"I'm sure there's a perfectly good explanation, Amanda." Betsy handed her the phone. "Call him."

"I have to welcome the counselors. But if you speak with Mr.—Detective Fleming, please be sure that he understands that there are children next door and he needs to keep his gun unloaded and in a safe place."

"Of course, dear. Give the children my best."

At ten, two small buses loaded with counselors pulled into camp. Dottie Roark had arrived shortly after breakfast to put the final touches on the infirmary. Amanda had talked her into taking on the role of nurse for the summer when the woman she'd hired fresh out of nursing school had called at the last moment to say she'd taken another job. Not that Amanda could blame her. Most of her staff came back summer after summer out of loyalty to her or because they believed in the work she was doing. It certainly wasn't for the money.

Dottie had left nursing to stay home with her children. Now that they were all in high school and working summer jobs themselves, she had some time on her hands and was delighted to help. It seemed that Amanda had barely hung up from offering her the position before Dottie was there, checking out the infirmary and ordering supplies.

The counselors poured out of the yellow school buses in a burst of noisy energy. They dropped their duffel bags in a pile and took turns hugging Amanda, meeting Dottie and catching up with each other. Most of them had worked at the camp at least one other summer. Some of them were former campers. Amanda's heart always swelled when she saw the returning campers because she knew it meant that Camp Good News had played some small role in changing their lives for the better.

"Mom sent you some of that apple butter you like so much, Ms. Hunter," one junior counselor said. "It's somewhere in my bag there. I'll have to dig it out and bring it up to the house."

"Hey, Amanda, the pier looks new! Watch this!" Jake Buntrock shouted as he ran to the end and pretended to almost fall into the lake. Jake was the camp clown, but he was also the best wilderness counselor Amanda could remember ever having at the camp. She wished swimming were part of his résumé because just a day earlier she had learned that Mike Connors, the counselor she'd hired to teach swimming, had been in a minor car accident. He was going to be fine but he needed physical therapy and it would be at least a month before he could get here.

"How's Miss Betsy?" Shari, the music counselor, asked.

"She's doing just fine," Amanda assured her, then clapped her hands to get everyone's attention. "Okay. Cabin assignments are posted on the dining-hall bulletin board and there are snacks to sustain you while you get settled in. Team meetings this afternoon, and of course, vespers and the campfire at sunset."

Amanda watched as the young people moved as one toward the dining hall, leaving behind them a trail of laughter and conversation. She smiled as she let the magic of their youth and enthusiasm wash over her.

"Dottie, I think it's going to be a good year."

Dottie linked her arm through Amanda's as they walked across the compound toward the infirmary and camp office. "Well, I know one thing," she said, "it's great to see you so involved again. These last couple of years—"

"Yeah," Amanda cut her off, not wanting to get into any discussion that could dampen her high spirits. "Well, the place isn't called Camp Good News without purpose, you know. Sooner or later, we all find our way."

Good thing I didn't come up here for peace and quiet, Pete thought as he put aside the novel he'd been trying to read. First the brakes on the old school bus had protested loudly as the driver negotiated the narrow winding road that led down to the camp office and registration area. Then the teenagers had piled out. Their voices had been muffled at first, drowned out by the bus. But once they hit the door, every word was at full volume and punctuated by the high-pitched squeals of the girls and the bass tribal grunts of the boys. And, of course, there was the dog barking out his welcome, apparently to each individual coming off the bus.

Pete reread the novel's first paragraph three times before he gave up. That was about the time the second bus arrived and the place exploded with a new volley of greetings shouted as if one party were on the other side of the lake instead of a mere two feet away.

"Oh, for goodness' sake," Pete grumbled and limped out of the boathouse and up the hill to the Bingle mansion.

"Pete!" Betsy Bingle waved to him. "Do come sit with us and enjoy the arrival of the children," she called. "The view from the veranda is perfect."

Pete immediately saw the folly of complaining about the noise and considered retracing his steps. But that would have been rude so he took several calming breaths and climbed the hill to the house. The twinkle in Betsy Bingle's eye told him he'd made the right decision.

"Come sit." Betsy indicated the wicker chair across from her own. A fresh burst of laughter and chatter penetrated the afternoon quiet. "Ah, now summer may begin. The children are here." She closed her eyes to savor the sound of them.

"How many of them are there?"

"In this group? Oh, perhaps a dozen. There are two young ladies—a music counselor and an arts and crafts counselor. They'll have the cabin with the youngest boys. Amanda has learned that the nine- and ten-year-olds still take comfort in a female figure. Then the young men counselors complete the roster and handle the older children—who can be a handful."

Pete frowned, but Betsy didn't seem to notice.

"Amanda sometimes has to make do and I believe she is a bit short-staffed this year." Her eyes flew open. "Do you swim, Pete?"

Pete was a little taken aback at the change in subject. "Yes, ma'am."

"Fabulous. Winnie!"

Winnie came around the side of the house, a garden hose in one hand and a pair of ancient lawn clippers in the other. "Yes."

"Pete can swim." She turned her attention back to Pete. "I am assuming that you are quite good at it?"

"Well, I don't like to brag, Betsy, but I was the state diving champion three years in a row in college." Pete relaxed, leaning back in the chair and stretching his long legs. The old lady might be a few cards short of a full deck, but she had a way about her that made a guy want to please her.

She clapped her hands together with excitement. "State champion. Imagine. And three times over! That's quite marvelous, Pete. Isn't he marvelous, Winnie?"

Pete grinned. "Thanks."

"Amanda will be delighted."

Instantly Pete was on alert. He sat up straighter and locked on the old woman's bright blue eyes. "And she would be delighted because…?"

Betsy ignored the question. "Winnie, remind me to

tell Amanda the news at vespers this evening." She turned her attention back to Pete. "Better yet, you must come to vespers with us, Pete. You can tell her yourself." She lowered her voice and leaned closer. "Oh, and you may wish to apologize for the incident with the gun earlier. I'm afraid she's quite stirred up about that. On the other hand, as soon as you tell her the news, all will be forgiven."

"Tell her what news?" Pete fought to maintain control over his exasperation with Betsy's impossible logic.

"Why, that you can take on the position of swim coach while you're here. The young man who was to hold the job was injured in an auto accident and can't arrive until later in the session. She's been frantic trying to find a replacement. She has the junior counselor, of course, but he struggled quite a bit as a camper and this is his first year as a counselor, so you're an answer to prayer." Once again, she applauded her idea.

"It's been several years since I was state champion or did much diving, Betsy," Pete began.

Betsy waved away his attempt at protest with a flick of her hand. "Nonsense. It's like anything else. It'll all come back to you the moment you're faced with the challenge."

"And there's my leg," he added.

"Pooh! Water therapy is all the rage these days. Swimming will speed the healing." She waited for his next objection, and when he failed to come up with anything more, she smiled.

"Now, dear boy, I'm afraid I must excuse myself. When you reach my age, you need a morning and an afternoon nap, especially if you plan to party into the evening." She punctuated that comment with a wink, then braced her silver-topped cane in front of her and rose with grace and dignity from her chair.

Pete leaped to his feet, his hand extended as if to prevent her from falling. She took his arm and beamed up at him. "Why, thank you, Pete. Just as far as the door will be fine, dear. Winnie and I will be by for you at quarter to seven. Vespers starts on the hour and we don't want to be late."

Chapter Three

Amanda loved the peaceful routine of the campfire vespers service. It was as if, after the sometimes chaotic activity of the day, everyone paused to take a breath. She always marveled at the way her counselors, so effervescent and adolescent throughout the day, grew still and serious as if they had gone deep inside themselves. Once the campers arrived, it would take no more than a few days for even the most rambunctious of them to fall into that same respectful quiet.

Everyone sat around the campfire on logs or blankets, watching the dancing flames, occasionally making a quiet comment to a neighbor. Amanda saw Winnie pushing Betsy in her wheelchair across the asphalt path Stan had built between the two properties. Pete Fleming trailed behind, looking decidedly uncomfortable, even from a distance of fifty yards. Amanda went to meet them, taking the measure of Betsy's houseguest in the process.

He was tall and muscular, but while his body was fit

and strong, his face was another matter. Pain was etched into every line that creased his forehead and the edges of his mouth. The dark circles beneath his blue-gray eyes told the story of a man who had not slept well in some time. She saw that if he smiled, there would be a dimple and that seemed incongruous with the rest of the man's demeanor. Up close, the limp she had noticed the night before seemed even more pronounced. But it wasn't just the limp. Pete Fleming moved like a man who had fought a hard battle and lost. Her experience told her that the battle was more than physical. She recognized a lost soul when she saw one. The fact that a man in that much pain had access to a gun was not a good thing, as far as Amanda was concerned. The fact that he had a gun and was living next door to her camp full of children was cause for major concern. When she realized that Pete Fleming was watching her with as much interest and scrutiny as she had given him, she stepped forward to focus all of her attention on Betsy.

As was her ritual, Betsy signaled Winnie to stop at the edge of the beach.

"Ah, Amanda, we begin yet another season," she called as Amanda approached. "Pete, would you be so kind as to let me take your arm the rest of the way?"

Amanda saw Pete's surprise when he realized that the frail older woman dressed to the nines in flowing purple chiffon and matching purple heels intended to walk across the sandy beach.

"Betsy, perhaps…" Winnie began but fell silent when Betsy waved her away.

"We have reinforcements, Winnie. Pete." She held out her hand and he stepped forward. Her smile was brilliant.

"And now, Amanda dear, here on my left," she instructed and Amanda took her place as she had for the last several years. "Oh, yes, introductions are in order. Amanda Hunter. Pete Fleming."

They gave each other a wary nod.

"Pete is fully prepared to explain the unfortunate gun episode of earlier, Amanda," Betsy continued, "so, as the children would say, 'cut him some slack.'"

"Ready?" Amanda asked quietly, ignoring the last statement. Betsy nodded and grimaced as they helped her to her feet. "Winnie is right behind you with the chair," Amanda assured her.

She felt Betsy's grip tighten on her arm and glanced over the head of the petite woman to Pete. She indicated that he should place his free arm around Betsy's back as she was doing. He did so and their arms met, crossing to form a makeshift chair back for Betsy.

Amanda smiled up at him and nodded encouragingly. The poor man looked terrified. "That's fine," she said softly and felt the slight release of tension in his arm as it touched hers. Or perhaps it was more that he had transferred the tension to her. Whatever the cause, she was inordinately aware of his bare skin against her own. It had been a long time since she had felt that particular prickle of awareness. She shook it off.

"Pete is not yet acclimated to the camping life, I'm afraid," Betsy was saying. "I warned him to cover himself with long trousers, but he has insisted on short pants. Ah, well, we shall see who was right after an hour on the beach with the mosquitoes. Winnie tells me they've come early this year because of the warm winter." Her words came in staccato bursts of information as she fought the toll that the exertion of the walk was taking.

"I have bug spray," Amanda assured her. "We can hardly have our guest attacked on his first night."

Betsy smiled and then stumbled a bit. Both Amanda and Pete tightened their hold. Winnie moved the chair an inch closer.

"Almost there," Amanda said softly. The counselors had all stood out of respect for Betsy. A few of the more senior counselors moved forward to greet her. Their youth and smiles of genuine pleasure at seeing her revived her and she straightened and covered the last few feet without incident.

As soon as she was seated again, Shari, the music counselor, began to play "Amazing Grace" on a wooden flute she had acquired on a mission to Central America. As the last notes trailed off, there were no sounds from the humans—only the crackling of the fire, the night songs of birds and the gentle lap of wave against sand as the wind blew across the lake.

The short service consisted of a reading by Winnie, followed by another familiar hymn, a long moment of silent reflection, followed by Betsy's prayer, then a final song as the sun disappeared behind the horizon. It was a first-night tradition that they had followed since Amanda was a child and a camper herself. It was like any tradition—Christmas, Thanksgiving—in that it reminded her of the goodness of her life and brought her a sense of peace and renewal. Trapped in her grief, she had missed so much the last two years. This summer she was determined to savor every moment and to make this the best season yet for her young charges.

During vespers, Amanda liked to look around the circle and study each face. It was a time when she knew she could see what was going on with her counselors and their charges better than any other part of the day. This first night, she saw only anticipation on the faces of her young counselors, contentment on the faces of her staff, and pleasure on the faces of Winnie and Betsy as they, too, scanned the circle.

She looked at Pete Fleming. He was seated on a log—Betsy had insisted that he take his proper place within the circle rather than standing back as an observer as he clearly would have preferred. He sat hunched forward, as if at any moment he might find it necessary to spring into action. Every muscle in his body was tense and at the ready. His expression was also one of wariness, as if he found himself in a circumstance he could not quite trust. He cast glances at some of the counselors, taking their measure and apparently not entirely pleased with what he was seeing. He was decidedly uncomfortable when Betsy began to pray. He did not bow his head. Just stared straight ahead into the fire. When the prayer ended and everyone joined hands for the final hymn, Amanda thought he might actually refuse, but fortunately he was seated between Winnie and Shari, and they took his hands without fanfare.

Then Amanda saw the first chink in his armor and a possible explanation for his tension. She saw him use the side of one sandal to scratch his ankle and then one shoulder suddenly jerked up toward his ear. She ducked her head to hide her smile. Betsy had warned him. The mosquitoes had come early and they had found a bountiful buffet in his unprotected skin.

Still, discomfort from a couple of mosquito bites didn't fully explain his tension or the way he had scowled as he studied the counselors. Out of the blue it occurred to her that what she was observing was that same defensive tough-guy persona she had seen dozens of times in the new campers during their first days. They were unsure of themselves in this strange environment, but doing everything they could to maintain their facade of control. As with any of her campers, her instinct to comfort and nurture Pete Fleming kicked in.

Then she caught herself. Pete Fleming was a grown man and Betsy's houseguest. Whatever his wounds, they were not hers to heal. In a few days the camp would be alive with adolescent angst and attitude, and she would have her hands full. Pete Fleming would have to work out his problems in his own way and his own time—as she had over the last two years. Besides, he had Betsy and Winnie to help him.

She joined in the final chorus of the hymn with gusto, squeezing the hands of the two counselors on either side of her. As soon as vespers ended, everyone resumed his or her normal chatter. Amanda stood and quiet was restored.

"Welcome to Camp Good News," she began. "Perhaps I should say 'Welcome back,' for all of you have been here before—either as a counselor, junior counselor or camper." She saw Pete Fleming resume his study of the group.

"Each of us has traveled a difficult road of our own and in a few days, we will have the unique privilege of helping others as they begin their journeys. For a few of them, these weeks at camp will not be enough even

to make a start. But for most, their lives will change—
at least for the time they are here. They will make fresh
discoveries about the world and about themselves, and
you will have the unique privilege of acting as their
guides."

She paused and allowed this to register. As usual the
junior counselors seemed more moved by her words
than their older counterparts, but everyone nodded and
kept their eyes focused on her.

"It's very important for you to remember that we are
an open community—if one of us is in trouble or pain,
then all of us have a responsibility to do what we can to
help. That is our creed here at Camp Good News."

She stood silently for a long moment. The only sound
was the crackling fire. Then in a very quiet voice, but
with a smile, she added, "Shall we have s'mores?"

Boo barked his approval of the idea as the circle
came alive. Everyone seemed to be talking at once and
the night air was filled with the sounds of their laughter and enthusiastic conversation echoing across the
lake. Several of the counselors gathered round Betsy
and Winnie to fill them in on events in their young lives.
Amanda and Dottie recruited some of the staff to help
bring out the makings for s'mores as well as coolers
filled with bottles of soda.

"Amanda," Betsy called. "Leave that to the others.
Pete here has some good news for you."

Amanda couldn't help noticing that Pete looked more
as if he were more likely to deliver a eulogy than good
news, but she made her way around the campfire and
joined the circle that surrounded Betsy.

"Well, tell her," Betsy instructed, then told Amanda

herself. "Our Pete here was a diving champion during his college days in Chicago. Three times over."

"That's lovely," Amanda said unsure of where this was going. "Are you originally from the Chicago area then?"

Pete nodded and slapped at a mosquito.

"Ha!" Betsy cried triumphantly. "I warned you. Winnie, get the spray from my bag there." Winnie followed directions and handed the bug spray to Pete, who hesitated.

"Oh, my goodness, is there a man on this planet who can admit he's been wrong? Spray yourself before the little darlings carry you off into the night."

"Well," Amanda said, preparing to get back to the counselors and their s'mores, still unsure of why Pete's swimming résumé was so important.

"Pete has agreed to take on the role of swim coach until the lad you hired gets here. Isn't that generous of him?"

Amanda stared from Betsy to Pete and back again. "That's very generous. But I wouldn't want to intrude on your vacation."

"Hardly a vacation," Betsy said. "He's on a sort of sabbatical and the interaction with youth is just what is called for. It certainly has worked miracles for you, Amanda."

Amanda glanced over at Pete who was looking at her with the same bewildered expression with which she was regarding him. "Well, obviously it would be a great help. Perhaps we can talk about it tomorrow?" she said, meeting his gaze and giving a slight nod toward Betsy.

She saw that he immediately grasped that she was giving him an out and relief flooded his handsome features. "That sounds like a good idea." He turned to Betsy. "May I help you back to the house?"

"In time. As soon as we've devoured our share of those delicious concoctions the children are preparing."

Pete looked at Amanda, obviously expecting support. Amanda shrugged and grinned. "There's no arguing with her when chocolate is involved. You may as well learn that right away. Come on. You get the sodas and I'll prepare the s'mores."

She was aware that some of the counselors grew quiet as she and Pete passed. They watched him even after he had retrieved the sodas and returned to Betsy's side. She did not miss the fact that one or two of the counselors seemed to recognize him.

"Betsy tells me you're a detective on the police force," she said as they sat on a log and ate their s'mores. "I believe she said that her nephew is your captain?"

"That's right." He didn't offer any further conversation, but concentrated on eating.

"That would explain the presence of the gun."

"Sorry about that. I—your dog— Look, can we just say that it was a mistake and won't happen again?"

"As long as the gun doesn't appear again, we might be able to do that. Were you feeling threatened by Boo?"

"Not exactly." He ate his s'more and looked around. "Where is your dog?"

She smiled at the deliberate change in subject. "Wherever there's the most likelihood of a dropped marshmallow or graham cracker. He's great at cleanup."

"These kids—I noticed you mentioned they'd been here before. Betsy told me you only take kids who've been in trouble."

"That's right." It was her turn to wait and see where the conversation might lead.

"And then you let them come back to be the counselors?"

"I hire the best of our former campers to come back and counsel. Most of them are eager to earn money for college, or in the case of the junior counselors, they've really had a good experience and they want to come back. They have to be enrolled in college and making decent grades before they can be hired as senior counselors."

His eyes followed one or two of the boys as they helped with cleanup.

"I understand that you and your family have been at this for some time."

"Well, my grandparents started the camp as a church camp, but then my parents decided that it could better serve boys between the ages of nine and fifteen who had been in some trouble or were borderline."

"And now you and your husband…"

"My husband died. I run the camp now with the help of some wonderful friends like Dottie Roark and her husband, Dan."

"I'm sorry for your loss." She didn't say anything, but was relieved to see that he knew a closed subject when he heard one. "Must be expensive," he said. "I mean where do these kids get money to go to camp all summer?"

"We have corporate and private sponsorships for those who can't pay the tuition—which is almost all of them. From time to time we get a boy from a so-called 'good' family—meaning they are upper-middle class who can well afford the fees." She nodded toward one of the counselors. "Jake's family, for example, has a summer home on the other side of the lake here. One of the new campers this summer has ties to the lake through his grandfather."

She took some pleasure in Pete's surprise. He looked over to where Jake was up to his usual antics, entertaining everyone with his talent for storytelling. "You're saying that kid was in trouble?"

"Actually, he was on his way to jail. He and a group of his friends had quite a little business in stolen goods when they were thirteen. It was only through the influence of his father that the judge agreed to have him come here for a summer."

"What happened?"

"He tested us at every turn, but we don't give up on these kids. They are first and foremost children, Pete, and the trouble they get themselves into is an outgrowth of something gone wrong in their lives. It's our job to try and break that cycle and reach out to them—give them some self-confidence and sense of personal pride and worth."

"You're saying all kids are good?"

"All children are innocents when they come into the world. We're the ones who corrupt them."

She did not miss his frown and knew that he didn't agree, but would be too polite to say anything more. He stood up and drained the last of his soda, then crushed the plastic soda bottle with one powerful grasp of his fist.

She stood, as well. "Why don't you stop by the office tomorrow or the next day so we can discuss the swim coach position?" Before he could protest or refuse, she walked away.

After everyone had enjoyed the treats, Amanda called them all together again around the fire. She motioned for another female counselor about the same age as Shari to come forward.

As Shari played taps quietly on her flute, the other girl signed the words. As the last note died away, the counselors slowly drifted back toward their cabins. Not a word was spoken, but Pete saw the young people smiling and signing to each other. Some of them were proficient at the language, while others were more awkward. Still, no one gave in to speaking aloud.

"What's with the sign language?" he asked as he pushed Betsy's wheelchair back to the mansion. His own voice sounded uncommonly loud after the silent retreat of the counselors.

"Isn't it lovely?" Betsy said. "Amanda started that tradition a couple of summers ago. She thought it would be a good way to offset the signing the boys pick up in their gangs. The young woman—Lexi, I believe is her name—anyway, Amanda was just delighted after hiring her to teach arts and crafts to learn that she knew signing."

Winnie took up the story. "She'll teach all of the campers to sign as part of their experience here. I think it's just the loveliest idea."

"It's nice," Pete agreed, "but these kids—well, forgive me but I don't see how learning sign language is anything they're likely to use."

"Oh, Pete, dear," Betsy sighed. "Not everything has to have practical value—although in some ways even this does. The point is that it's a way of assuring that at the end of the day, there will literally be peace and quiet. As the campers settle in for the night, they will have this brief respite from the need to talk."

"Amanda calls it 'reflection time,'" Winnie added. "It does wonders for the boys, and it's also good for restoring order. If there's too much hoopla, all Amanda or any of them have to do is go silent and sign and magically, chaos is gone."

They had reached the house. Pete did the only thing that made any sense to him. He lifted Betsy in his arms and carried her inside while Winnie folded the chair and stored it in a hall closet.

"Why, Pete, how gallant of you." Betsy's eyes twinkled.

"Where to, my lady?" Pete asked, enjoying the fact that something so simple had delighted her so.

"To my chariot there at the foot of the stairs, kind sir." She pointed to a chairlift that ran along a track up the wide staircase. "Winnie will take care of things from there."

He did as she asked. It was impossible not to notice how delicate and frail she was beneath the layers of chiffon.

She made a gesture. "That means 'Thank you,' Pete."

"Now you go like this," Winnie instructed showing him another sign.

He gave it a try. "You're welcome?"

Both old ladies nodded vigorously.

"And now, dear Pete—" Betsy made another sign. Winnie repeated it and mouthed "Goodnight."

Pete imitated the gesture and left, pulling the door firmly closed behind him. He stood for a moment looking up at the stars and enjoying the stillness.

Out here, it was as if he had stepped into a completely different world. It wasn't real, but for now, it wasn't a bad place to be.

Amanda shouldn't have had time to give a moment's thought to Pete Fleming, and yet she did. It wasn't that he was around. In fact, during that first week, she barely saw him. But she certainly heard about him.

"Dan says the guy staying at Betsy's is really nice," Dottie commented one afternoon when she and Amanda were alone in the office.

"Hmm," Amanda said, and concentrated harder on the list of chores she was developing for the campers to follow.

"He certainly seemed nice enough the other night at the campfire," Dottie went on. "Quiet though—in a kind of dark mysterious brooding sort of way, don't you think?"

"I hadn't noticed. What do you think the chances are that the campers can be depended on to do their own laundry every week?"

"About the same as they are for me getting you to admit that you've noticed Detective Tall, Dark and Brooding," Dottie muttered and went down the hall to the infirmary before Amanda could respond.

Even Dan seemed to find it necessary to fill her in.

"Saw that detective guy in town today," he commented one evening when he stopped by to be sure everything was set for the arrival of the campers the following Monday. "Pete," he added.

Did he think she'd forgotten the man's name? Did he think that between Dottie and Betsy and Winnie and him there was the slightest chance she might forget the man's name?

"Had coffee with him."

"That's nice," Amanda replied noncommittally and checked off another item on her clipboard.

"He won't say much about how he got shot but I have a feeling it's tied to his coming here."

"So Betsy has indicated," Amanda said, still not looking up from her list.

"I think he's a pretty lonely guy, but when I asked him to come for supper, he turned me down—nice about it. Said maybe some other time—you know, the way some folks do when they mean that it probably won't happen?"

Amanda gave up. The only way she was going to get through to Dan was to acknowledge the subject. "Well, according to Betsy, he's come here for a little R&R. My guess is he wants to just focus on healing and getting himself ready to return to work."

"Yeah. I got that impression. Still, he strikes me as a guy in a world of hurt. Just wish we could do something for him."

Then there was Betsy. Every day Amanda got a full report on Pete Fleming's activities.

"The poor dear hobbles along the path at break of dawn each morning, but I think his leg may be improving. Such a dangerous job, police work, unless, of course, one has a desk job as my nephew, Rudy, does."

Amanda knew she was supposed to ask for more details, but she tried changing the subject instead.

"The counselors are settling in. It's going to be a good year in spite of some gaps in the—" She stopped herself but not soon enough.

"Ah, the lack of an actual swimming coach to work with that young Turner child. Have you spoken to Pete about that?"

"Not really. After all, Betsy, his injury may prevent him from swimming and he may be too self-conscious to admit it."

"Nonsense. He's swimming every afternoon. I suspect he has developed his own routine for rehabilitation for his wound and clearly, swimming is a major piece of it."

Amanda opened her mouth to respond to that, but Betsy had yet another thought. "Besides, it's not just about the swimming, Amanda. The man is on the opposite side of the law from your young charges. He has been shot by someone like them. Let them see for themselves the realities of the path they are on."

"Betsy, I know you're just trying to help—both Detective Fleming and Camp Good News—but I think we have to respect the fact that he came here to get away from his work. Throwing him in with our boys will only remind him of what he's trying to forget."

"Or it could be the very thing he needs to put things in perspective. He can always refuse the position, Amanda."

"I'll speak with him," Amanda promised, knowing she couldn't win.

"Excellent."

But it was her nightly walks with Boo that were the biggest problem. She had a choice, of course. She could choose to go away from the boathouse instead of past it, but that way was more congested because houses had been torn down to make way for condominiums and the path was frequented by more people walking their dogs or out with their kids. This was her time of day to unwind. Besides, when she went the less-populated route, she didn't need to keep Boo on a leash.

"I mean," she said to Boo, "it's not like the man is going to want to invite us in or anything."

But she couldn't help being aware of him as she passed the boathouse. She couldn't help seeing him through the kitchen window as he stood at the sink. She couldn't seem to help herself from taking note of where in the house he was on her return walk an hour or so later. Sometimes the boathouse was completely dark except for the loft. Sometimes the car would be gone and she'd wonder where he went.

"Which is none of my business," she said to Boo and picked up the pace.

A couple of nights she was simply too exhausted to take her usual walk. On those nights she would let Boo out and watch him run straight down the hill and through the bushes. She always assumed he wandered along the path, sniffing out his favorite places before returning. Then one night he returned and she discovered pizza sauce around his mouth. And the next night, she found tiny pieces of carrot in the fur of his paws.

After Betsy and Winnie both denied leaving treats for the dog, Amanda decided to let Boo run free but follow him. As she should have suspected, he made straight for the boathouse. By the time she got there, he was nowhere to be seen.

Then she heard the low murmur of a man's voice. She followed the sound around to the deck of the boathouse.

Pete Fleming sat with his back to her. Boo sat at attention near his feet. Occasionally he would place one paw on Pete's knee as if to be sure he had the man's attention.

This is too good to miss, Amanda thought and stepped farther into the shadows.

"So you plan to make a habit of this, do you?" Pete Fleming said.

Boo sat at his feet, tail wagging, watching him closely for any sign of a treat.

"I ate out tonight, big guy, so no leftovers."

Boo remained seated, refusing to give up. He shifted slightly, perhaps to make sure Pete didn't get distracted.

"Hey, I'm telling you there's no food. An apple. There's an apple. Do you eat fruit?" He stood up and went inside. Boo followed.

Amanda felt a little like a Peeping Tom, but nonetheless she eased closer.

Pete stood at the counter cutting an apple into slices. Boo watched every move.

"One piece and then you're outta here, pal."

Boo's tail had thoroughly polished the floor where he sat. Now he stood on hind legs and gently took the piece of apple from Pete's fingers.

Pete chuckled softly and smiled. "Now get outta here."

Boo resumed his sitting posture.

"Nope." Pete shoved a piece of apple into his own mouth and walked to the door. "Go on."

Amanda slipped quickly around the corner of the house. She heard the door slide open and waited for Boo to come around the side of the house. Then she heard Pete say, "All right, one more."

Amanda covered her mouth to keep from laughing out loud. Boo had conquered the tough detective. She managed to make it back to the path just as Boo came around the side of the house.

"You little scamp," she said softly as he trotted proudly alongside her, the apple still firmly in his teeth. "Maybe Betsy's right. Maybe getting the detective involved with the boys would be good for everyone concerned."

Boo was more intent on hanging on to his apple than he was in listening to her, but that didn't stop Amanda.

"I mean, if he gets to know them then he can't help but understand that their problems are hardly their fault. It will make him a better detective—more understanding, don't you think, Boo?"

Boo had given up trying to save the apple until they reached home. He was lying on the grass savoring the treat.

"Oh, Boo, Betsy is right. You men are all the same—absolutely no patience."

Chapter Four

By the end of the week, Pete had settled into a routine. He rose before dawn and walked the trail along the lake. It was more of a workout than he had first imagined. An old law on the local books required that every lakefront property owner provide access for a pedestrian path along the perimeter of the lake. Some had taken this more to heart than others. In places the trail was well maintained, even paved, while in others the property holder clearly was determined to discourage passage. Pete liked the challenge of it. He was determined to work up to a light jog as soon as possible.

After making his own breakfast, he spent the morning tackling the tangled gardens, clearing brush, trimming bushes and raking out the flowerbeds. By noon, he was ready for a swim followed by lunch and then a nap, which he took lying on the pier next to the boathouse. His afternoons were less structured. Sometimes, he'd go into town on an errand for Betsy or Winnie. Sometimes, he'd sit out on the deck, intending to read, but observing the goings-on at the camp next door instead. Before dinner, he would swim or use the canoe stored in the lower part of the boathouse. Whatever his activity throughout the day, his intent was always the same—exhaustion. So far it had worked. He had not had the dream once since that first night.

He had also managed to avoid dinner at the mansion, not wanting to have to answer Betsy's questions about his role as swimming coach for the camp. And he had managed to avoid a repeat of the vespers routine by staying in town past sunset. But now it was Saturday and the counselors were given a free night—their last free night for six weeks. When he'd returned from his morning walk, Winnie had greeted him with this news, warm muffins and an invitation to come to dinner. He couldn't think of a single excuse not to go.

Now he lay on the pier and squinted up at the sunspots, drifting between sleep and stupor. He would have been completely unaware of Amanda's approach if it hadn't been for the jingle of Boo's dog tags. Pete stayed where he was, his hat low over his face, his body perfectly still, until Boo started licking his ear and he couldn't restrain a twitch.

"I thought we should talk about the swimming thing," Amanda said sinking into a sitting position next to him with her bare toes kicking the water. "Betsy's sure to bring it up at dinner tonight."

He heard the snap of a pop-top can and raised himself to one elbow, pushing his baseball cap into place. She handed him a can of lemonade, and popped a second for herself. The dog lay down between them as if fully prepared to join the discussion. He looked up at Pete with questioning eyes.

"Look," Pete began, "I just don't think—that is, I'm not good with kids." Especially troubled kids.

"I thought you worked with young teens in Chicago?"

"I'm a cop, Amanda, not a social worker."

"You're also a good swimmer, judging by your afternoon marathons. And then there's that state champion diver feature." She grinned. "Come on. I could use the help."

He hesitated and realized he didn't want to disappoint her. Still, there was no way he could see himself getting so directly involved. "I thought you had another kid in mind," he said.

"Rob is a junior counselor. He has his certification, but he got it in a city pool. He's not used to a big lake, and he's only just turned sixteen. It wouldn't be fair to him or the campers to put him fully in charge of the program."

"What if I agree to be there for the sessions—in the background—just in case?"

Her smile put the sun on the sparkling water to shame. "And you could coach Rob—behind the scenes, of course. Give him pointers on how he might do things better?"

"Well, yeah, I guess."

Boo rolled onto his back and pawed the air as if the whole thing were settled.

"Thanks," Amanda said as she stood up. "I really appreciate this, and I promise you that as soon as Mike, our senior coach, can get here, he will."

It seemed rude to remain seated while she stood. Besides, it was disconcerting looking up at her. Her legs were way too bare, too long and too close. He struggled to his feet and as soon as he did, she stood on tiptoe and kissed his cheek. "Thanks so much. You've really made my day."

She and Boo ran across the lawn to the camp while Pete tottered on the pier, trying hard not to lose his balance and fall into the lake as he watched them go. Just before she reached the sand beach of the campgrounds, she turned and waved. "I'll send Rob over to introduce himself and give you the schedule," she called. "See you at dinner."

To Amanda's surprise, Rob was less than thrilled with the news that Pete had agreed to mentor him.

"This is the guy from the campfire the other night?" he asked as he concentrated on jamming one toe into the soft sand, refusing to meet her eyes.

"Yes, and he was a state champion diver."

"Like a hundred years ago or what?"

Amanda smiled. "Well, it probably wasn't more than fifty years ago. He's still a pretty good swimmer."

Rob continued his study of his shoes.

"Look," Amanda said, "I know you thought maybe this was your chance to move up to senior coach, but…"

"That ain't—isn't it," he muttered.

"Then what?"

"He's a cop."

"And?"

"He's *the* cop—the one who arrested me three years ago before the judge sent me here."

"I see."

Rob looked pleadingly at her. "He's got a rep for not liking kids, Amanda. How's he gonna be my coach when he hates kids like me? Probably hates kids period."

"This is different. When he arrested you and others, he was doing his job. You had done something wrong— seriously wrong."

"And?" Rob asked in a perfect echo of her earlier question.

"And, this is different. You're not in trouble. He's not on the job. You're on neutral ground—a good place to start over. In fact, you can show him how much you've grown and changed. You might actually teach him a thing or two about not giving up on boys like you were. What do you say?"

"Looks like I got no choice," Rob replied, gloom dripping from every syllable.

Amanda wrapped her arms around him. "You always have choices, Rob. The trick is to make the right one. You could quit, which would solve the problem of having to face Mr. Fleming, or you could give it a chance and see what happens."

Rob looked up at her. "And then quit if it goes bad?"

"If it goes bad, we'll work something out. How's that?"

Rob smiled. "Works for me. When am I 'sposed to meet with this dude?"

"I told him you'd stop by with the schedule."

"Now?" Rob was clearly horrified.

"No time like the present," she said and handed him the printed schedule of camp activities with the swimming sessions highlighted in yellow. Then she turned him toward the boathouse and gave him a little push.

"The sooner you meet the dude, the sooner we'll know how things are likely to go."

"Yeah, I know—a journey of a thousand miles and all." He trudged off as if prepared to meet his maker.

Amanda watched him go. "*Lord, let it work,*" she whispered, "*for both of them.*"

Pete answered the door, half expecting Winnie, half hoping for Amanda. When he saw the tall African American teen, he tensed.

"Robert Turner, or is it still Silky?" he said.

"It's Rob. Just Rob."

"I thought I recognized you the other night." He made no move to invite the boy inside.

"Yeah, I was kind of surprised to see you, too." He shifted from one sandaled foot to the other. "You gonna let me come inside or what?"

Pete took a step back, leaving enough room for Rob to walk past him. "I'm not here to make trouble for you," Pete said, "unless you give me cause."

Rob bristled. "That a threat or what?"

"Let's call it a warning."

Rob shrugged and turned away from Pete's hard stare. "Nice place." He walked across the room to stare out at the lake. Pete waited. After a long moment Rob turned and headed back for the door. "This ain't about to work," he muttered. "No way."

He opened the door, but Pete slammed it with one open palm. "Try me. Why are you here?"

Rob continued to look anywhere but at Pete as he fished in the pocket of his shorts and produced a folded paper. "To give you this. Amanda sent me—it."

Pete opened the paper and saw the schedule for swimming sessions for the summer. "You're her swim counselor?"

Rob straightened defensively and glanced at Pete. "Yeah."

"Does she know our history?"

"Yeah. I told her. She don't care."

"How long have you been doing this—teaching kids to swim?"

"A year at the Y."

"Are you any good at it?" Pete saw that the question surprised Rob.

"Amanda don't hire nobody but the best," he boasted.

Pete studied the schedule, buying time. He could not believe that he was actually considering this. "How's your mom?"

For the first time, Rob dropped his tough-guy facade. "Still sick with the cancer," he said softly.

"I'm sorry to hear that," Pete replied and meant it. Ella Turner had done her best for Rob and her three other children, working three jobs, trying to stay one step ahead of the bill collectors, and fighting breast cancer for the last three years. "You want something to eat?" Pete nodded toward the bowl of fresh fruit that Winnie replenished every other day for him.

Rob took an apple and polished it with his two large hands.

"Well, sit down and let's talk about this," Pete said indicating the sofa while he took the chair and spread the schedule on the table.

Rob hesitated, then sat and took a bite of the apple. "We have two sessions a day—morning for swimming and afternoons for a free swim. That's more of a life-guard thing."

"You have the whole camp at one time?"

Rob shook his head and pointed to a column on the paper. "Nah. It goes by age. See? Monday and Wednesday is the little kids. Tuesday and Thursday, the older ones."

Pete nodded, then left the paper on the table and leaned back, studying Rob. "You were in a lot of trouble last time I saw you. You didn't have much of a future."

"Yes, sir."

"What happened?"

Rob shrugged. "I got before the judge and Mama was there and she told the judge she'd heard about this place and begged him for me to get sent here being how I was only thirteen."

"So the judge agreed?"

"Not right away, but Amanda come racing in at the last minute right when the judge was asking Mama about how she expected to pay for camp and keep me there when I wouldn't even stay in school." Rob smiled at the memory. "She was something—Amanda. Walked right to the front of the courtroom and made her case for me—she didn't even know me. Mama wrote her a letter and she just showed up. I never saw anything like that in my life. Mama calls her our angel."

"So you came here?"

"Yeah, last two years as a camper and then this year as junior counselor. If I do this right and finish high school and get into a college somewhere, I could come back as a real counselor next year after I graduate high school."

Pete was startled. He'd known kids like Rob Turner his whole career. Most of them didn't plan beyond the next hour, much less a year into the future. Maybe he *had* changed.

"So you want my help or not?" Pete asked.

The cautious, defensive attitude was back. "Depends."

"On what?"

"On whether or not you're gonna trust me to do the right thing or just be waiting for me to mess up."

"Trust has to be earned," Pete replied. "In our history, I don't have a lot of evidence that I can trust you."

To his surprise, Rob grinned. "That's exactly what Amanda used to say."

Pete picked up the schedule and stood. Rob was on his feet at once, and Pete realized it was something he'd been taught and now did without thinking.

"How about this?" Pete said, offering Rob a dish for his apple core. "I'll meet you down at the beach at six tomorrow morning. You show me your plan for teaching these kids. We'll run some trials to see how strong a swimmer you really are, and then we'll decide."

Rob hesitated for half a second, then stuck out his hand. "Okay."

This was ridiculous. Amanda could not decide what to wear. She hadn't given much thought to this sort of thing for years. She had certain clothes for certain occasions, certain seasons. Yet here she stood staring at the contents of her closet as if she'd never seen any of it before.

For some reason she couldn't quite fathom, she was considering wearing a skirt instead of her usual dressier slacks. Betsy liked her dinner guests to be a bit more formal in their choice of dress—although Betsy preferred to think of it as more traditional. She could not abide jeans or shorts at the dinner hour, but she was fine with a pair of freshly pressed slacks and a dressier blouse or sweater. So why on earth was Amanda putting on a dress and her sandals with the little bit of a heel?

Pete Fleming.

The man's face flashed across her mind as she stood before the bathroom mirror applying lipstick and mascara. Her cheeks flared with color, almost as if she'd missed her mouth and colored her cheeks instead. Boo watched her, his head cocked to one side in a quizzical expression.

"Well, maybe it's a healthy thing. He is a good-looking man and the fact that I've actually noticed is probably just evidence that things are getting better for me, don't you think?" She tissued off half the lipstick, then changed from the heels to flat sandals. Boo followed her to the kitchen where she filled his bowl.

"No, you are not invited. This is a grown-up party." She picked up the salad that was her contribution to the meal and left.

As she walked the path that ran through the grove of tamarack trees between her house and the Bingle estate, she heard Betsy and Winnie laughing. Then she heard Pete's soft baritone and the clink of ice against a glass. They were in Betsy's sunroom, and all the windows were open.

"Ah, at last," Betsy exclaimed when Amanda arrived. "And don't you look simply fabulous, my dear?" Betsy smiled knowingly and Amanda felt the blush creeping up her neck to her cheeks.

She turned away and found herself face to face with Pete. The man was checking her out. It might have been some time since any man had looked at her in that appraising way, but a woman knows that look.

Well, who would have suspected? Amanda thought as she looked for some way to ease the moment—to get things back to normal. She twirled around, showing off the full-skirted dress. "I thought I would surprise you by not wearing pants for a change. Do you like it?" she asked Betsy.

"It's quite smashing, my dear."

Amanda saw Betsy glance at Pete and then smile. "Yes, absolutely the perfect thing," Betsy added.

"I remember how much Stan loved it when you wore a skirt or dress," Winnie said as she poured Amanda a glass of lemonade. "He used to say…"

Betsy interrupted, changing the subject. "Pete has offered to grill steaks for us, Amanda. And he does the potatoes and corn on the grill, as well. The man is a gourmet cook."

"Aw, shucks, ma'am, it's just a steak," Pete replied. "And speaking of that, I'd better check the fire. Ladies, if you'll excuse me."

As soon as Pete was out of earshot, Winnie sat next to Amanda and took her hand. "I am so sorry to have brought up Stan, Amanda. I mean, it's just that you look so lovely and Stan—"

Amanda patted the older woman's hand. "It's fine, Winnie. It's perfectly fine for you to talk about Stan. I hadn't thought about that in a long time, but you're right. I remember that twinkle in his eye whenever I got dressed up a bit."

"Well, the one with the twinkle tonight was our handsome young detective," Betsy said.

"Betsy, I don't need a matchmaker," Amanda replied gently. "And I most definitely do not need a summer romance. You've been reading too many novels."

Betsy and Winnie both laughed. "Guilty," Betsy admitted.

"But you can't deny that he's really the most appealing man," Winnie gushed. "I mean in a dark, brooding sort-of-Heathcliff way."

"I think the vernacular of the young people these days would be to say that our detective is 'hot.'" Betsy put a breathless, husky emphasis on the last word.

This sent all three women into a fit of giggles just as Pete returned. He stood at the door, looking decidedly perplexed. "I'm ready to cook," he said, sending all three women into another outbreak of the giggles.

"I'll get the steaks," Winnie said, fleeing the room, her hand pressed to her lips.

"I'll toss the salad," Amanda said and also left the room.

Pete looked at Betsy. "Was it something I said?"

Betsy ignored the question. "It is such a delight to hear Amanda laughing again. The poor woman has had her share of pain these last years. You two have a great deal in common, I suspect. You should take some time to get better acquainted."

Winnie returned with a tray filled with the steaks and vegetable shish kebabs, and handed it to Pete. Without a word, she returned to the kitchen.

"These won't take long," Pete said.

"Lovely. I'll go check on everything else and send Amanda out to give you a hand," Betsy said. "I thought since it was such a lovely warm evening, we could eat out here on the porch."

To Amanda's relief, Betsy had obviously decided to stop matchmaking by the time dinner was ready to serve. The conversation settled into a more normal pattern. It revolved around the upcoming season for the camp and was liberally peppered with fond memories of the days when Amanda's parents and grandparents had managed the camp.

Pete was mostly quiet, but he seemed to enjoy the evening and the conversation. Once or twice Amanda was aware of him looking over at her with interest.

After they had finished the meal with ice cream sundaes, Betsy stifled a yawn. "Pete, dear, would you be so kind as to see Amanda home?" Betsy asked after they had finished their dessert. "I have an early doctor's appointment in the morning and I really must get my proper rest."

"I can…" Amanda began, but was interrupted by Winnie.

"Goodness no, Amanda, there's no need for you to help with cleanup. You and Pete are our guests. I'll see to it. You two young people run along."

The choice was to accede to the obvious attempt of the two ladies to throw them together or to make more of a deal of things by arguing the point.

"Actually, I'd appreciate the company," Amanda said and smiled at Pete.

They said their farewells and walked the short distance between the two houses in silence. Amanda couldn't help but smile at the contrast in style. There was Betsy's elegant mansion, and less than a hundred yards away stood the log home her grandparents had built as the appropriate rustic landmark for the camp. She loved this house: its warm light visible through the small-paned windows and the wide expanse of the front porch with bent twig furnishings her grandfather had created during the long winters.

"Would you like a cup of coffee?" she asked when they reached the bottom of the steps to the front porch.

"I would," he said, and it surprised her. "Unless you were just being polite and thought I'd refuse." He was smiling.

"I keep forgetting you're a detective. Guess I'd better watch my step."

"So do I get the coffee or not?"

"Sure. Come on. Do you want decaf?"

He made a face.

"Ah, that would be a 'no.' One cup of the real stuff coming up. I'm going to assume you take it black?"

"Now who's the detective?" he replied and held open the screen door for her.

"Make yourself comfortable out here. If you light those lanterns, the mosquitoes won't be a problem. Matches are there on the banister in the planter."

In addition to making the coffee, she took a moment to check her hair and makeup, but stopped short of doing anything about either. She also decided against the more formal tray and accessories. She added cream to her mug before pouring coffee in both mugs and then carrying them out to the porch. Boo trotted along at her heels, eager to check out their guest.

Pete stood at the railing staring out at the lake. At the sound of the door opening, he turned and relieved her of one of the mugs. She led the way to two of the chairs pulled close to the edge of the porch. She sat and propped her feet on the railing. He grinned and followed her lead. They each took a long swallow of their coffee.

"Good stuff," he said. "Thanks."

The silence between them turned awkward. Amanda searched her brain for some topic of conversation. They'd already covered his swim-coach duties during dinner.

"Tell me about your husband," he said quietly.

If she had been quiet before, she was speechless now. Of all the topics he might have introduced, this one was the last she would have expected.

"Stan? What do you want to know?"

"What do you want me to know?"

She resettled herself in the chair, curling her legs underneath her. "Well, he was a good man. A decent and kind man. A gentle man."

Pete nodded. She couldn't really see his features, but she knew he was watching her. He waited for more.

"The campers adored him. There was nothing he couldn't or wouldn't do." She smiled at the memory. "Sometimes Betsy used to say that Stan was the biggest kid in camp."

"How did he die?"

She felt the shock of remembering wash over her as it always did. For a moment she was angry. How dare this veritable stranger ask such a question?

"He drowned," she said and stood up. "More coffee?" Her tone left no doubt that this time she was only being polite.

Pete stood and handed her his empty mug. "No, thanks." He walked to the steps that led to the yard. "I could take Boo for a walk, if you like."

Boo raked his paws against the screen in reply. Amanda could not help but smile. "You don't have to," she said.

"One thing you'll learn about me pretty fast, Amanda, I'm almost never doing something just to be polite. If I make an offer, I mean it."

Her smile wavered. She wondered if there was some underlying meaning in his words. Now who's been reading way too many novels? "I'll get his leash." Boo followed her.

She returned with the dog leaping at her side and straining against the leash. "It doesn't have to be a long walk," she said. "In fact—"

He took the leash from her. "Got it," he said and turned to go. At the bottom of the steps he turned back. "Look, if I was out of line asking about your husband, I'm sorry. Betsy said it's been a couple of years and…"

"I loved him," Amanda replied quietly as if that explained everything.

Pete nodded. He walked away without saying anything more, the dog tugging at the leash, pulling him down toward the water.

"The counselors will be back soon," she called after him. "They have curfew. One of them can bring him home."

Pete waved and kept walking.

Chapter Five

An hour later, Pete was headed back along the path toward the camp. Boo was content to walk at his side, no
longer pulling at the leash or exploring every sound and
smell. Pete saw a car moving slowly down the gravel
drive that skirted Amanda's house and led to the mess
hall and other common buildings of the camp. He
wouldn't have thought much about it except the headlights were off and it was obvious that every effort was
being made to go unnoticed. He pulled Boo into a
wooded area that gave him a good vantage point and
waited.

The car stopped next to the mess hall. Someone got
out on the passenger side and opened the back door.

"Shhh," the boy ordered whoever was in the back seat.

This was answered with barely suppressed giggles as
the back-seat passenger emerged and collapsed against
the other boy.

Now the driver got out and hurried around the car to
help support the one from the back seat.

"I'm gonna hurl," the back-seat boy announced with no attempt to keep the news quiet. The other two leapt back in horror and the boy fell to his knees and vomited.

Pete moved closer. Boo was at his side, on alert but quiet as if sensing the need for surprise. Pete could hear the driver and other passenger arguing in whispers as they debated a plan. The boy on the ground continued to heave. Pete got within three feet of them and then reached into the car and flicked on the headlights. He said quietly, "Is there a problem, boys?"

The two boys standing shielded their eyes from the glare of the headlights while the kid on the ground moaned.

"We're toast," the driver said and held up his hands in surrender. Pete saw that it was Jake—the kid whose family had a place—and apparently a car—here at the lake.

The kid from the passenger side took a step forward but halted as Boo let out an impressive growl and pulled at the leash. "No problem, sir," he blustered. "Robbie's just got some kind of bug."

"Then perhaps we should head on over to the infirmary," Pete said.

"Our very thought," Jake said, and the other kid nodded. Pete recalled how Amanda had mentioned that the kid was a born storyteller.

"You could have just driven him there, but you probably were having trouble seeing. That's why they put these lights on the car—for night driving."

The two boys were silent while the one on the ground lurched to his feet. When he turned, Pete saw that it was Rob Turner. He took little satisfaction in realizing that he'd been right all along. The kid was trouble.

He caught Rob by the shoulders before he pitched forward. "You're drunk," he said, and Rob grinned at him.

"Inishiasion," he slurred. Then he stood at attention and saluted. "Counselor Rob Turner reporting for duty, sir." Then he twisted free of Pete's grip and threw up again.

Pete knew he was overreacting but he was angry. Just that morning, Rob had been waiting for him at six, had demonstrated impressive skills in the water and had been equally impressive in his plans for managing the swim sessions. Now here he was drunk, sick and laughing about it. Pete had gotten suckered in by the manners and intelligence, but the kid was just like the ones he'd left behind in the city. He knew how to play the game when adults were around.

"Whose idea was this?" Pete demanded.

The others looked at each other. "Well?" Pete said.

"It's a rite of passage, sir. You know, the new kid. We gave him one beer, honest." Pete began recalling other bits of information about Jake, who was obviously the ringleader. Apparently, in addition to his theatrical skills, he was an excellent negotiator.

"Do I look that stupid to you guys?"

They had the good sense to look abashed. "No, sir," they muttered.

Just then two other cars rolled into the camp. The occupants appeared to be returning from a nice evening out as car doors slammed and there was the normal laughter and chatter of kids saying their goodnights. Lights went on in cabins up and down the row, but Pete noticed that two or three of them never entered a cabin. They edged closer to the mess hall.

"Jake? Everything okay?" The girl who Betsy had introduced as the music counselor stepped around the side of the mess hall and froze. Shari, Pete recalled, and it felt good to know he hadn't lost his talent for remembering details.

"Apparently not," Pete replied. "Come join us and have your friends come, as well. We're going to get to the bottom of this."

Shari bristled. "We can handle this," she said. "No need for you to get involved."

"Or get Ms. Hunter involved?" Pete asked. "I don't think so, kids. Seems to me that I heard every one of you agree to a certain code of ethics the other night at the campfire. Seems to me that code's been violated."

"Sir, couldn't we work something out?" Jake pleaded. "I mean there's really no harm here. So Robbie got a little smashed. He's paid for it. He's pea-green sick."

"You see, that's not my problem. My problem is that he's underage so let's talk about how he got smashed— who was involved, what choices he might have had, what choices you guys had, that sort of thing. Now the way I see it, each of you knew this was happening and yet it doesn't look like you did much to stop it."

He paused and looked directly at each of the teens now standing in the light of the car. "We can either do this the honorable way and you can own up to what went down tonight, or we can do it the hard way while you try to cover your own backsides and put the blame on somebody else. Your choice."

To his surprise the first response came from Rob, who was still holding his stomach and slouching against the building. But ridding his system of the alcohol had gone a long way toward sobering him up.

"It was my idea," he said and struggled to his feet. "I asked them to get me the beer."

Pete did not miss the way the others glanced nervously at each other. "I see," he said. "Still, everyone here had a choice in this."

"I made them, man. Leave them alone." Rob's voice was firmer now. "Deal with me."

"I think you should all go to your cabins and get some sleep," Amanda said as she stepped out of the shadows and into the light. "I'll deal with all of you tomorrow once the campers have arrived and are settled in."

There was no arguing with her although she did not raise her voice. In fact, Pete thought, she might have been discussing the weather, so calm and even was her tone. The counselors trudged away. Rob held back.

"I can't let this pass, Rob. You know that." Rob nodded. "Go on," she said softly, and with a last glance at Pete, he followed the others.

"You can turn off the spotlight now," she said, pointing to the headlights. "We don't have time for a dead battery on top of everything else."

Was it his imagination or was she annoyed with him? He reached inside the open car door and flicked off the lights.

"Now then, let's get one thing straight," she said, her voice coming at him from the sudden darkness. "I have been dealing with incidents like this one tonight for years. I appreciate your help, but I know what's at stake. I'll handle this, okay?"

"Look, I saw the car coming into camp with no lights on. What was I supposed to think?"

"This isn't the inner city, Pete. There's no need for you to be constantly anticipating trouble."

As his eyes adjusted to the night, he saw her more clearly. Everything in her body language told him that she was upset and apparently she was upset with him.

"Suit yourself," he muttered and headed across the campground to the boathouse. Halfway there, unable to let the matter drop, he turned back. "For what it's worth, the kid, Rob, is covering for the others. I never would have expected it from a kid like that, but he is."

To his amazement, she laughed. "I won't argue the first part, but you've got a lot to learn about these kids, Detective, and you need to start from the idea that they really don't enjoy being bad. I'll make sure Rob is there for the first swimming session tomorrow. Can I tell him to expect you, as well?"

Pete was still digesting her sudden change in mood. "Yeah, okay," he said and walked away.

"Goodnight, Detective," she called after him, her voice as gentle as the night breeze.

"Stop calling me that if you don't want me acting like one," he replied and trudged on, realizing that he must surely resemble the chastened teens.

The arrival of the season's first group of campers was always an event. If vespers were Christmas Eve, this was Christmas Day—long anticipated, eagerly prepared for, and then suddenly here. Amanda knew that the time she would have them would go far too quickly. All too soon they would board the buses and head back to their real lives in the city. The only hope she had was that she would send them back with a little kernel of hope, of inspiration for making better choices and working harder to change the lot they'd been given.

With the staff and counselors, she was there to meet the buses as they rattled down the winding gravel road and released their contents of nine-to-fifteen-year-old boys. There was a lot of noise, a lot of confusion and a lot of attitude.

"Try and make me," a short stocky boy shouted when Jake tried to check his backpack.

"Aren't you Antwone Richards?" Amanda asked, coming up beside him. "The basketball player?"

The kid's bravado faltered slightly. "Yeah. So?"

"Well, it just seems to me that anybody who's as good at a sport as I've heard you are would know that every game has rules. Play by them or you're out of the game."

Antwone's face reflected confusion, but he remained belligerent.

"The backpack," Amanda said quietly, never taking her eyes from his. "That's a rule here. We check it or you're out of the game." She looked down at her clipboard for a second. "According to this, if you get tossed out of this game, you end up in juvie back in the city. Your choice, Antwone. There's the bus." She turned and walked away.

"Got me some important stuff in there," she heard him say.

"You'll get it back when you leave," Jake assured him.

Antwone heaved a dramatic sigh. "Sounds like jail either way—some choice." This last was shouted in Amanda's direction.

But Amanda barely heard the boy's retort. She was more aware of the fact that Pete Fleming had elected to trim bushes between the camp and Betsy's property at this specific moment. She had no doubt that he was using the yard work as a cover to observe the arrival of the campers. She wondered how many of them he might recognize, how many he might have arrested or inter- rogated at some point. Maybe getting him involved in the activities of the camp was a mistake. She realized he was watching her, realized that she had paused and was staring across the campground to where he stood in the high bushes, and did the only thing she could think to do. She smiled and waved as if he were a fa- vorite neighbor. He turned back to his work attacking the bushes with a frenzy.

"Manda! We've got trouble." Mary from the kitchen staff hurried to catch up with her. "Edna's cut her thumb—could need stitches. Dottie took her to the emergency room. Grace and me can't finish lunch and get it served by ourselves."

"Okay." Amanda changed direction and headed for the mess hall.

"Oh, yeah. Almost forgot. The showers in cabin four are stopped up."

"Okay." Amanda continued on to the mess hall. The showers would have to wait.

Stay out of it, Pete commanded himself as he whacked down another impressive stand of buckthorn. She told you flat out, so just let her figure it out for herself.

Whack. Whack. Whack.

But the last kid to emerge from the last bus was none other than Travis Sanders—gang name Cockroach. By any name, Travis Sanders was trouble. At fifteen, he had a sheet longer than a lot of convicts twice his age, and he was a rising leader in one of the most dangerous gangs in the city. The gang leader was known only as Joker. Pete and his partner had been trying to nail that guy for the last year. They knew that Joker was not from the neighborhood. Joker was educated and middle to upper class. Pete was sure of it. And Travis was in Joker's gang. Travis Sanders was way beyond anything Amanda was prepared to deal with—Pete would bet his badge on that.

You have to tell her—make her understand. At least make her aware.

Whack.

I'll keep an eye on the kid.

Not good enough. She needs to know.

She won't like me butting in.

Whack.

What if something happens?

Whack. Whack. Whack.

Pete growled audibly and dropped the hedge cutters onto the ground. He wiped his brow with the back of his forearm and stared across the compound. He watched Travis meet his counselor, Jake. He saw Jake offer a firm handshake and a ready smile, saw Jake throw a welcoming arm around the camper's shoulders. Travis gave him a fake grin and returned the handshake, turning it into some ritualistic process that made Jake laugh. Obviously, Travis knew how to play the game.

"That's it," he muttered and started across the compound. "Where's Amanda?" he asked the first staffer he saw.

"Could be in the mess hall or if she's not there try cabin four—the showers are down in there."

Pete nodded his thanks and headed for the mess hall. The dining area was quiet and deserted. He crossed the length of the large room and pushed through the double doors leading to the kitchen where chaos reigned.

Pots were bubbling, a couple of women were frantically peeling and chopping vegetables. Amanda was pulling loaves of slightly scorched bread from a giant oven and shouting out commands.

"Somebody stir that spaghetti sauce before it boils over," she yelled.

Pete was closest to the pot. One of the women chopping stuff for a salad passed him a long-handled spoon and nodded encouragingly. He stirred.

"What else?" the woman chopping salad called out with a grin at Pete.

"Now throw the pasta into that kettle there—the one with the boiling water and cut the fire a little."

She continued to wrestle with the hot loaves of bread, banging the pans against the counter to dislodge them.

With the sauce semiunder control, Pete turned his attention to the pasta. He dumped the noodles into the boiling water, causing it to foam over the lip of the pot and sizzle on the stove.

"Cut the fire!" Amanda shouted and raced to take over.

The look on her face when she saw him was priceless, and in spite of himself, Pete grinned. He reached down and twisted the control to Off.

"Fire cut," he said and noticed how the two other women nudged each other and grinned as they watched Amanda.

He had to admit that he was enjoying this. For the first time since he'd met her she was speechless. On top of that, her short, side-parted hair kept falling over one eye and she kept trying to blow it out of the way. She looked more like one of the campers than the owner of the place.

"Well, not all the way off," she said finally, and focused on resetting the heat. "Mary or Grace can take it from here."

"They look pretty busy," Pete replied, nodding to where one of the women was now tossing the salad and the other was removing fresh-baked cookies from a cookie sheet to a platter. "Do you want me to handle the spaghetti or slice the bread?"

The campers could be heard on the other side of the double doors, talking at that extra-decibel level common to boys of a certain age and scraping chairs across the wooden floor.

"You go do the welcome and say grace with them, Amanda," one of the women said. "We've got this."

Amanda looked skeptical but headed for the door. Pete turned his attention back to the spaghetti and sauce.

"How are you with fixing clogged showers?" she asked, her hand resting on the door.

Pete glanced over and grinned. "About as good as I am at this," he replied and the other two women laughed.

"Mary. Grace. Pete Fleming." Amanda made the introductions with a nod at each of them in turn. "He's staying at Betsy's."

"Well, bless his soul, he's surely welcome today," Mary gushed. "Now, honey, you take care of slicing those loaves and I'll handle the sauce, okay?"

Amanda rolled her eyes and pushed open the door, raising the volume on the clatter of the hungry boys beyond.

"I know you don't want to hear this," Pete said later that afternoon as she handed him tools and he repaired the shower.

"But?"

"But you've got a boy in this group who could be major trouble for you."

Amanda sighed. "You're right. I don't want to hear it. Don't even tell me his name or anything else."

"He's dangerous, Amanda."

"He's a boy just like all the others. He's had a hard life and he's made some poor choices, but I guarantee you that he thought they were his only choices."

"Still, you need to keep an eye on him." He tightened the head back into place and wiped his hands on a rag.

"I know you mean well, Pete, but if I single out one of the boys, then it says I doubt them all. There has to be a certain level of trust or the camp just won't work. These are smart kids. Even if I didn't mean to, I would find myself paying more attention to this boy. He would know it. The others would know it. It sends the wrong message."

"Even if it means putting yourself or others at risk?"

"What's he going to do? There's nothing here worth stealing. If he overtly acts out then he's out of here, and if he's as bad as you think, then chances are he's come here as an alternative to being sent to reform school. The opportunity to turn this kid's life in a different direction is way beyond the risk. Trust me. He's not the first boy we've had here who's on the edge."

"Betsy has plenty of stuff worth stealing and she's right next door."

Amanda grinned. "Ah, but she has you and you know who the kid is and presumably he knows you, so unless he's totally stupid he's not likely to try anything, right?"

He didn't want to tell her all of it—there was no reason to scare her. He'd just have to keep his eye on Cockroach, in case his coming here was some kind of a setup for Joker to pull something.

"What about your other neighbors?" It sounded like what it was—a last-resort argument.

This time she laughed out loud. "Pete, every house on this lake is alarmed to the hilt. If your young man gets within ten yards of any house here—including Betsy's—believe me, somebody will know about it." She finished packing the tools in her father's battered toolbox then glanced at her watch. "Thanks for helping out here, but the first swim lesson starts in five minutes."

"Did you have a chance to talk to Rob and the others?"

She tapped her watch. "Four minutes," she said. "I really stress that the staff set the proper example by not being late."

"You could have just told me that it's none of my business," he grumbled as he held the door for her and they emerged into the bright sunlight.

"It's none of your business," she said and smiled as she said it. "Antwone? Haven't you forgotten something?" she called out to the boy trudging down the path.

The kid gave her a blank look and impatient what-now sigh.

"Your towel?"

"Don't got one," he muttered and looked to see if anybody else was around to hear.

Amanda went to him and put one arm on his shoulder. "It's 'I forgot to bring one, Ms. Hunter.'" She steered him in the direction of a storage room. "Fortunately, I have extras."

Antwone looked at Pete. His expression asked for help. Pete just shrugged. "Come on, kid. We're both in hot water here. Let's get those towels and get down to the beach."

It was not a good session. Rob was nervous and self-conscious. Pete was impatient and anticipating a screw-up. Amanda once again considered that she might have made an enormous mistake by involving Pete Fleming in the activities of the camp. Her zeal to help anyone in pain had overshadowed her good judgment. The last thing she needed was some messed-up police detective second-guessing her every decision with the children.

He was a nice enough guy and her instinct told her that his heart was in the right place. On the other hand, his experiences with boys like this were different from hers. He saw them at their worst, on their own turf where they would risk everything—even death—to remain cool in the eyes of their peers. She got to see them a little off guard, on unfamiliar ground. It gave her an advantage. Before they could recover from the culture shock of this camp on a lake in Wisconsin, they were caught up in the routine of camp life. They were even enjoying it.

"Not like that," she heard Pete yell.

Rob turned his back on Pete and said something to

the boys in the class. They nodded and tried the exercise again. Pete paced the shoreline, dragging his wounded leg noticeably.

Amanda started toward the beach and then stopped. She saw something familiar in Pete's agitated movements. She'd seen it before. Dozens of times. Pete Fleming was dragging around more than a wounded leg. He was carrying a boatload of anger in every step. And, unless her years of counseling had been for nothing, Amanda would be willing to bet that for some reason that anger was directed inward and had very little to do with the kids.

"Okay, that's it for today," Rob said. "Change and head on over to Shelter One for crafts."

The boys scrambled out of the water and ran past Amanda, their towels wrapped around their bony shoulders. A few of them offered her high fives as they passed her. Obviously, from their point of view the session had been a success. She saw Rob come out of the water and approach Pete. Pete made no attempt to meet him half way, but stood with arms folded and head down, knowing the boy was coming his way.

Instinctively, Amanda moved in to interrupt, but before she could, Rob reached Pete. Amanda paused and held her breath.

"These are the little kids," Rob said. "I know what I'm doing out there."

Pete made no response.

"Hey, man," Rob continued. "I know I messed up the other night. Amanda and me worked it out. I don't owe you, but Amanda says part of being a man is stepping up—like clearing the air and stuff."

Pete looked directly at him. They were about the same height. Rob was thinner, but at the moment, he looked more the man of the two of them. Amanda could not move. She was fascinated to see what would happen next.

"So I'd like to apologize and ask you to get past that. I'm a good swim coach—especially for the little kids. They like me. They—"

"They respect you," Pete said in a voice so low that Amanda had to strain to hear. "That's worth a lot more."

Both of them relaxed slightly.

"You want some pointers with the others? The older guys?"

"Yeah. Sure. Mama has this saying—something about a horse and the mouth. I'm not sure—"

"Not looking a gift horse in the mouth?" Pete guessed.

Rob smiled. "Yeah. That's it. I don't know what she means by it, but if she was here, she'd be saying it now. She's always saying it when somebody offers to help—'specially if it's somebody she don't much like."

To Amanda's surprise, Pete laughed. "Well, kid, you always did speak your mind."

They stood there for a minute sizing each other up. Then Pete held out his hand and Rob took it. They shook and Rob headed for his cabin, passing Amanda as he did. He nodded politely but said nothing.

Chapter Six

After a week, Pete hardly noticed the noise coming from the camp. He sat on the deck of the boathouse and worked on notes for Rob to use in teaching swimming. Finally, he set the notebook aside and walked over to the side of the deck that faced the camp. Rob and a couple of other counselors were storing the canoes and paddles for the night. It had taken courage for Rob to come to him and apologize for the drinking episode without Amanda sending him.

Considering everything, Rob's first swim session with the older boys came off fairly well. He was nervous, but then so were the kids and it all evened out. Pete couldn't help but be impressed with the way Rob handled a couple of the boys who refused to pay attention. He just stood quietly and pretty soon the other boys all turned their attention to the boys who were misbehaving. Peer pressure was a powerful weapon. As soon as the rebels realized that the others didn't think their actions were all that cool, they settled down. When they did, Rob continued the lesson.

Pete wondered if he'd learned that from Amanda. It took guts just to stand there, not saying anything. It was a risk, because if the others enjoyed the misbehavior then he'd lost them all. When Rob started the lesson again and glanced over at Pete for the first time, Pete had given him a subtle thumbs-up. The rest of the week's sessions had gone equally well, and Pete found himself looking forward to the next session.

The scent of food cooking drifted across the compound. Almost time to feed the little monsters. The cook's hand was still bandaged so Amanda had put her to work in the camp office. That meant that Amanda was still short-handed in the kitchen. He had nothing special on his calendar. Might as well lend a hand.

"Pete!" Mary and Grace greeted him in unison as soon as he entered the kitchen. Amanda wasn't there.

"Ladies." Pete found an apron, folded the bib top down and then tied it around his hips. "What's cooking?"

They giggled and indicated the menu written on a whiteboard near the door. "You and Grace get these pans of chicken and potato wedges out to the warmers," Mary instructed, "I'll finish the corn on the cob and get the biscuits."

"Where's Amanda?" Pete asked Grace as they carried the flat pans out to the serving table and set them on warmers.

"She's got enough to handle. Mary and I told her we could make do until Edna can get back."

"And you think that will be…?"

"Oh, tomorrow or the next day for sure. You won't be able to keep her out of the kitchen for much longer.

Edna's been cooking for these kids for over eighteen years now. She wouldn't want to let Amanda down."

"What about you and Mary? How long have you been here?"

"Every summer for the last twelve. We retired from the public school system ten years ago and missed the children. Working here gives us the chance to be with them. We even get to do a little teaching."

"Really?"

"Oh, yes. Everybody at Camp Good News pulls double duty. Amanda's grandparents always believed that the kids should see people in different roles. That way they learn not to stereotype and judge. Her folks carried on with it. Ah, here's Amanda."

Pete glanced up and then wiped the palms of his hands nervously on the apron.

"Well, Detective, you are just a wealth of surprises, aren't you?"

"I just thought that with Edna still out of commission and..." He was acting like a schoolboy with a giant crush on the teacher. "I stopped by to see if the ladies needed help. It's not a regular thing."

"But he sure looks good in that apron, right, Amanda?" Grace gave him a wink as she returned to the kitchen.

"I really appreciate it—everything," Amanda said as she took another apron from a hook and put it on. "We can manage from here if you have other plans."

Pete picked up a pair of tongs and held them over the chicken pieces. "And miss the opportunity to try this incredible-smelling chicken? Nope, I'm here to serve and then to eat."

"And not a minute too soon," Mary announced as she

pushed open the double doors with one hip and carried out a tray of corn on the cob, followed closely by Grace with a platter of hot biscuits. "Here they come."

A stampede of wild horses could not possibly have made more noise. Apparently a couple of weeks of camp activities was more than enough to put the boys at ease with each other. The junior counselors were not much quieter, wanting badly for their charges to like them and look up to them as cool. The senior staff seemed well used to the hullabaloo and made little effort to control the level of noise.

Everyone went to a table designated for that cabin; senior counselor at the head of the table and junior counselor at the foot. They all stood, and gradually the chatter subsided.

A staffer sounded a bell and in unison the boys said grace. Or rather the counselors and returning older campers said it and the new campers shifted uneasily from one foot to the other.

The "Amen" was barely said when the room erupted once more. Plates clattered as the boys lined up to get their meal, chairs screeched in protest and forks clanked against china as they reclaimed their places at the table.

Pete quickly got into the rhythm of serving, depositing two pieces of chicken on each plate as it came by.

"I'll take that breast and thigh there," Travis Sanders said pointing to a far corner of the pan very close to where Amanda stood serving the potatoes.

Pete didn't have to see the leer on the kid's face to get the insinuation directed at Amanda, but before he could open his mouth, Amanda spoke.

"Here at Camp Good News, all food is blessed and

sustains us, Travis." She reached over and removed the baseball cap he was wearing at an angle that signified his gang affiliation. "Like everyone else, you'll take the next piece—whatever that might be. Perhaps you'll try to get to dinner on time and stand a better chance of getting the piece you want."

She plopped a spoonful of potatoes on his plate and turned her attention to the next person in line.

So she had noticed. Pete was impressed. Travis had been fairly sly in the way he'd entered the mess hall a few minutes after everyone else. He'd waited for the prayer and then come in just as everyone was lining up, blending into the crowd. Pete had seen a perp do the same thing a thousand times. He'd also seen the look Travis gave Amanda once she'd chastised him. He turned to say something to her, but saw that Amanda was watching Travis even as she continued to serve the other campers.

Pete felt relieved. She'd figured it out for herself. No need to keep harping on it. He turned his attention back to serving chicken.

Rob was next in line. "Nice job today," Pete said as the boy accepted the chicken.

Rob looked surprised, but muttered his thanks and moved on. When his plate was full, he doubled back.

"You got a minute to talk about something?" he asked Pete. "I mean—no big deal or anything."

"Sure. Any time."

Rob hesitated as if he wanted to say more, but instead just shrugged and walked away.

"What was that all about?" Amanda asked.

"Beats me. I figured you would know. Maybe it had to do with the incident the other night."

"That's all handled."

"And you're not going to fill me in on the details?"

"It's a private thing between me and the boys. Let's just say that it won't happen again—at least until next year." She grinned and put down her spoon. "Well done, Detective. I think we got them all served in record time. I hope you'll stay and eat with the staff." She was dishing up a plate for herself as Mary and Grace already had.

"A man's got to eat," Pete said and filled his own plate before following them to the table for senior staff.

As they ate, Amanda observed Pete and the way he easily fell into conversation with the rest of the staff. He asked good questions—questions that had people telling him stories about their lives. He was an excellent listener, focusing all of his attention on the person speaking.

He must be very good at his job, she thought. I'm sure I would tell him everything I knew if he focused those eyes on me and flashed that dimple in appreciation or interest.

Eat, she ordered herself and turned her attention to her food, stealing occasional glances at Pete. It was hard not to notice how the lines and shadows she had noticed that first night were slowly disappearing. Or how his exposure to the sun had taken away the pallor of those first days. She hoped that he was healing as well on the inside, but somehow she doubted that. His suspicion of the boys—especially Travis Sanders—indicated that he still found it hard to believe that these children could change.

Yes, she had known all along that he was trying to warn her about Travis. It was irritating the way he seemed to assume that she was some novice in need of his protection while working with these kids. On the other hand, he had come to the rescue more than once— at least in terms of providing another badly needed pair of hands to help with the work. He glanced over at her and gave her that half smile of his. That smile—she had thought about that, too.

Why not let it go? Why did he hold back? It was one of the most revealing and attractive things about him. Attractive? Well, that was certainly not what she'd meant—it wasn't attraction she felt. It was interest, curiosity, but definitely not attraction. The man interested her the same way a child she couldn't quite find the key to would interest her. She certainly wasn't—

"Earth to Amanda," Dottie said softly, giving her a nudge.

Amanda blinked and turned quickly to her friend. "I'm sorry. I wasn't listening."

Dottie gave her a wry smile. "Nope, but you sure were looking." She stood up, and before Amanda could protest her statement, she added, "I'm heading back to the infirmary. See you later?"

Amanda quickly gathered her own barely touched plate and stood, as well. "I'll come with you." She had to nip in the bud any idea Dottie might have about an attraction for Pete Fleming. She had her hands full just trying to keep Betsy and Winnie under control on that score. She placed her dishes on the dishwasher belt and hurried to catch up with Dottie.

* * *

It wasn't until the following day that Pete remembered Rob had wanted to talk to him about something. The kid was quieter than usual as they set up for an afternoon relay the older kids would take part in as part of their swim session.

"Something on your mind?" Pete asked as they laid out the course.

Rob shrugged and checked the diagram on his clipboard. "Just something I noticed. It's probably nothing."

"I've learned that it's a good idea to trust your instincts, especially if the thing troubles you."

Rob glanced over at him. "There's this kid in our cabin. He's pretty slick."

"Meaning?"

"He says and does all the right things, but there's just something about him that makes me—I don't know—edgy around him, I guess."

Cockroach, Pete thought. "Have you mentioned this to anybody else? Isn't Jake the senior counselor in your cabin? Amanda seems to think he's pretty sharp."

There was a long pause. "Yeah. I know she does. Could be just me, you know."

"Maybe." But Pete didn't think so. Something the boy had observed had raised his suspicions.

"It's just there's this younger kid in the cabin and he's not like the rest of us—not from the streets like us."

"Okay. Is there a problem?"

"Well, I think somehow the other guy is working the kid. You know, getting him thinking that he needs to keep this other kid happy or pay a price."

"Then maybe you should say something—either to

Jake or if you don't want to do that, mention it to Amanda. She'd keep you out of it."

"You know," Rob went on, "if I said something and he got in trouble when he didn't do nothing, then—well, the others would know I was the one."

Ah, the law of the street—honor among delinquents. Rat out another and pay the price.

"Well, it's a tough place to be. I'll give you that. Still, if something's in the works, Rob…" Pete deliberately left that hanging to see Rob's reaction.

Rob shook his head. "It's not that. I mean there's nothing concrete. Just a feeling."

"Do you want some advice?"

Rob nodded miserably.

"Keep your eyes and ears open. Trust your instincts. If you think this kid is up to no good, chances are you're right. You just need a little hard evidence."

Rob looked at him with noticeable relief. "That's a good idea. You know, Amanda says we can't single anybody out for either good or bad, but she'd want me to keep an eye out for trouble. That's what a counselor does."

"But you need to talk to somebody about your concerns."

"I'm talking to you," Rob said, his eyes piercing as he stared hard at Pete.

"Yeah, but I don't work here."

"That's the reason I told you and not any of them. You're not one of them but you're hanging around a lot and maybe you could keep an eye out with me. See if you don't think there's something."

For the life of him, Pete could not imagine why he didn't tell the kid to leave him out of it. Why instead he nodded and said, "Yeah, I could do that. On one condition."

Rob waited for the deal.

"If you hear or see anything concrete, you come to me at once. Don't try to handle it on your own."

"Deal," Rob said. "Do you want the names?" It was clear that he would be hesitant to give them.

"No need to put yourself in that position. I'm pretty sure I know."

Over the next two weeks, Amanda watched Pete become more involved in the daily life of the camp. He spent more time with Rob, coaching him on teaching new swimming techniques or sometimes just talking as they sat together on an overturned canoe near the water.

At first, she had flattered herself that she was the attraction. Pete certainly seemed to turn up when she least expected him. But she pushed that idea from her mind and looked for other reasons for his coming around even when there was no need. The truth was that she wasn't ready to deal with the fact that after two years of mourning, she felt this little spark of interest in another man.

She was relieved when she decided that his interest was in the kids. It was evident that they fascinated him. It was as if he couldn't believe that something so simple as getting them out of their natural environment and giving them the opportunity to just be regular boys could really make a difference. Amanda knew that it did. Summer after summer, she had seen it work. Oh, they wouldn't save every boy. Some of them—like Travis— would return to the old ways within days of leaving the camp. But her father had once told her that even if all they did was change the life of one boy each summer, they had done God's work and that was all He asked.

There was one thing about Pete's interest in the camp that troubled her. Chad Devereaux was an excellent diver. There was no question of that. But he also had refused to associate with the other campers from the outset. Lately, Pete had taken note of the boy's diving talent and taken him under his wing. That only made things worse.

She definitely needed to talk to Pete about that. She looked up and saw the man himself shouting directions to Chad. The boy listened, nodded and then executed a perfect dive.

"Well, no time like the present," she said aloud and headed for the beach. "Chad," she called, her voice carrying across the water, "your cabin starts the ropes course in twenty minutes. Better get changed."

Chad looked at Pete, who shrugged. "You heard the boss." Reluctantly, the camper dove into the water and swam for shore. Once there, Pete handed him a towel.

"Good work today, kid. Stop by later and I'll loan you that book on diving we were talking about."

Chad nodded and walked past Amanda and up the hill toward the cabins.

"He's really talented," Pete said.

"Yes, well, we need to talk about that," Amanda replied and sat down on a fallen tree, patting the seat next to her.

Pete grinned. "I feel like I'm being called to the woodshed," he said as he sat beside her—a little too close beside her.

She ignored that. "How are things going with Rob?"

"Fine. You were right. He's come a long way. Of

course, he gives you most of the credit. Why? Is there a problem?"

"Not with Rob." Amanda shifted positions and cleared her throat. "It's about your relationship with Chad."

"I'm just offering the kid a few pointers." His tone was immediately defensive.

"You're making it possible for him to separate himself from the others. I can't allow that."

"I thought you wanted me to get involved."

"You can't pick and choose."

"Look, this kid is—"

"Not like the others. I'm well aware of that." How dare he patronize her! She stood up, seeking an advantage. This was not going well. "Perhaps you can tell me exactly what you think you're doing to help him."

Pete blinked up at her. "I am coaching him in his diving," he said, enunciating each word as if he were speaking to a two-year-old. If he had added the ever-popular "Duh!" she could not have been responsible for her actions.

"You're doing more and you know it."

"He's lonely and out of his element here. The other kids had his number five minutes after he got here. Rich kid whose daddy bought him a light sentence. Well, now he's on their turf with no rich father to protect him. They smell weakness and believe me, they will go for the jugular."

"Oh, really, Pete, stop talking like something off a TV cop show. This is serious."

Pete threw up his hands in exasperation and stood. "Look, make up your mind. You got me into this. Rob doesn't have the skills to help Chad with his diving, so I stepped in. I thought you'd be pleased."

They were practically toe-to-toe which made it necessary for Amanda to tilt her head back in order to look up at him. "I appreciate everything you're doing—"

"But?" His tone was challenging, then his expression softened. "Look, maybe I am getting a little overinvolved with this one. Truth is, he reminds me of myself."

Amanda's natural concern for the boy in the man kicked in. "Well, that explains a lot, but—"

He laid his fingers on her lips and smiled. "Another 'but,' Amanda?" Then he laughed nervously. Reluctantly he took his fingers away from her mouth. "Look, let's have a bargain. I'll ease up and encourage him to be more a part of the group."

"What's my part of the bargain?"

"You give me a little credit for knowing what I'm doing." He held out his hand to her.

She shook it firmly. Together they turned and started back up toward the office. "Can I tell you a little about Chad?"

"Sure."

"You're right about his background being pretty different from the other boys. His grandfather owns a large summer home at the other end of the lake."

"That's not something he wants the others to know."

Amanda nodded. "He told you?"

"We've talked about a couple of things. I made some lucky guesses. He opened up. For the record, I believe him when he says he didn't know the others were involved in buying drugs."

"His parents indulged him shamelessly, excusing his

early run-ins with the law as the normal actions of a high-spirited youth. And then he was arrested and convicted when they found the drugs on him."

"I've had years of experience with these kids, Amanda. Those drugs were planted. He was out on a lark—underage driving, maybe a beer—were his greatest crimes."

Amanda gave him a skeptical look. "Perhaps. The bottom line here is that Daddy's money got him placed here instead of locked up. It's our job to make sure that—"

There was that grin again—crooked, reluctant, flashing a dimple that made him look anything but tough. "*Our* job, Amanda? I'm flattered."

"You're impossible," she said, her cheeks pink with pleasure. "Just take it easy with him, okay?"

Pete saluted, then watched her head back to the office.

When Pete returned to the boathouse, Chad was there waiting for him.

"Aren't you supposed to be at the ropes course?"

"I cut out." There was no attitude in the words, just the blanket admission. The boy sat on the step, his elbows propped on his knees, his hands cupping his face as he studied the ground intently.

"That doesn't fly with me, Chad. You can't decide what you will and won't do in this place. You have to play by the rules like everybody else."

Chad glanced up at him and then back at the ground. "Some don't play by the rules. They just don't get caught."

"And if you didn't want to get caught, why come here to my place?"

"I need to talk to you."

"Whatever it is can wait. Now, come on." Pete took the boy's arm and pulled him to his feet. He felt no resistance.

"Yeah, okay." He headed back toward camp, his shoulders slumped, his hands in his pockets.

"I'll catch up with you after supper at vespers. We can talk then."

"Whatever." Chad did not look back.

Pete watched him go. Perhaps Amanda had a point. Maybe the kid was becoming too dependent on him. He'd have that talk with him after supper.

"Pete!" Betsy Bingle's quavering voice rang out across the lawn. Pete looked up toward the mansion and waved. Betsy was seated on the patio and she motioned for him to come up and join her. "Winnie has deserted me. Come, have some iced tea."

"Be right there," he called back and went inside the boathouse to get a book he'd borrowed from her library. The book was on the nightstand in the loft. He stopped for a moment before picking it up, his senses on instant alert.

Something was different in the room. The bed covers were smooth—maybe too smooth? The drawer to the nightstand was closed tight, as were the dresser drawers and door to the small closet. But the closet light was on. He opened the door cautiously, half expecting someone to be inside although he'd heard nothing.

The contents appeared undisturbed. Pete stripped off his T-shirt and tossed it in the hamper as he looked around. He pulled a polo shirt off one of the shelves and put it on, still looking for something amiss. He automatically felt along the back of the top shelf for his service revolver. He'd put it there after that first day. It was still there. He shut the light off and started to close the closet door when he noticed a trace of something on the carpet.

Sand.

He always removed his shoes at the door and left them there. In this room, he was either barefoot or walking around in socks. Winnie had come just the day before to do her weekly cleaning—a ritual that she insisted on even though she repeatedly commented how neat and tidy Pete kept everything. When Winnie cleaned, she did it with gusto. There was no way she would have missed vacuuming the carpet.

Pete searched for other clues, but found nothing more than the few grains of sand. "You've been away from the job too long," he muttered as he picked up the book and headed out the door. That sand could have been there for months or it could have fallen off your T-shirt just now—you were at the beach, sitting on that log with Amanda.

"And you were in a rush this morning. You probably left the light on," he told himself as he walked up to the mansion. "Stop jumping at shadows already."

"Well, you didn't have to change on my account, Pete, dear."

"Wanted to make a good impression on you," he replied with a grin, the incident at the boathouse already forgotten. He helped himself to iced tea and refilled her glass, then took the Adirondack chair next to hers.

"You seem to be getting more involved with things at the camp," Betsy observed.

"I like staying busy and I've run out of bushes and weeds to attack over here."

Betsy smiled. "Yes, you did approach that task with a certain amount of vigor. There were times when Winnie was a bit concerned—for the plants and for you. Fortunately, the plants will grow and thrive. How are you doing?"

Pete was not expecting the twist. When he looked at Betsy, he saw that she was entirely serious.

"Better," he admitted. "My leg has come a long way. Thank you for letting me come here."

"Oh, Pete, you hardly need to thank me. Surrounding myself with young people like you and Amanda is what keeps me going." She paused to take a sip of her tea. "How are things going with Amanda?"

Pete knew exactly where this conversation was headed. It was the reason she'd called him up to the patio. Betsy wanted an update on her attempts at matchmaking.

"You'll have to ask Amanda that question," he replied evenly.

"Now, Pete, do not be coy with me. I have decades on you and the two of you are not fooling me for one minute. You like her and she likes you—that is established. I am asking if things have moved beyond that— as you very well know, Detective."

Pete laughed and realized how normal it felt. How normal all of this felt—sitting on a patio enjoying a conversation with a friend on a summer afternoon. How long had it been since he'd left the job at the station and really taken the time to enjoy a moment like this?

"Pete?" Betsy prompted.

"Okay, an update. At the moment, Amanda is a little upset with me. She thinks I'm taking too much of an interest in one of the campers."

"Chad Devereaux," Betsy replied with a nod. "She's right, you know."

"How do you know Chad?"

"I was courted by his grandfather and when I chose another suitor over him, he was quite upset. He had a terrible temper. And then there's the boy's father—rigid and cold to his very core. No wonder the boy acts out. He's practically screaming for attention and the only way he gets it with his father is when he strays from the straight and narrow, I'll wager."

Pete was amazed at her grasp of the details of Chad's life.

She sat for a moment staring out across the lake, then continued. "His grandfather owns that monstrosity at the far end of the lake there. Nothing would do but that Walter Devereaux have the biggest, showiest place on the lake." She stared at the large ostentatious house for a long moment. "One can buy almost anything except good taste and happiness, wouldn't you agree, Pete?"

"Tell me more about Chad," Pete said.

"Sad case. Always skipping school as I understand it and that has put him behind and given him something of a reputation as not so bright. His father was top of his class throughout school and finished summa cum laude at Yale, then went on to pursue both his MBA and law degree. That's a lot for a small boy to measure up to."

"So when he got into trouble, his father pulled strings to have him land here?"

Betsy looked shocked at his statement. "Goodness me, no. His father never came to the court at all. It was Amanda who brokered the deal to get him sent here in-

stead of someplace harsher. I think he might have reminded Amanda a little of her son. Danny would be
about the same age now."

Pete thought he must have misunderstood. "You're
saying Amanda has—had a son? A kid of her own?"

"Oh, I was sure I mentioned that. Didn't I? Yes, I'm
sure I did. Danny. He drowned the same night as Stan did."

Pete couldn't believe it. He'd assumed that she had
only had to deal with the loss of her husband. That was
more than enough. But her kid, too? It took longer than
two short years to get past something like that. How was
she putting one foot in front of the other, much less running this camp?

Betsy stared out at the calm sparkling water. "She
talks about Stan, but never about Danny."

"You think she blames herself?" Pete asked as much
to himself as to her. The information Betsy had given
him explained a lot and at the same time raised more
questions.

"I think she has been trying very hard not to blame
God," Betsy replied.

Pete nodded. He didn't want to get into a theologi-
cal debate with Betsy, but he knew for sure that if the
two people he loved more than anyone else died at the
same time, he'd have questions about God's purpose—
that is, if he believed in God.

Betsy reached over and touched his hand. "Well, now
the question remains of whether or not you're too dense
to pursue the woman romantically. I do remain hopeful
that you will offer her your friendship in the remaining
weeks you plan to be here. She needs a friend like you—
someone who has known his own share of pain. Some-

one who can listen and not try and tell her everything will be all right. It will, of course, eventually. God sees to that, but even He would have short patience with some of the patronizing drivel that poor woman has had to endure these last two years."

A car door slammed and Betsy got to her feet. "Ah, Winnie's back. I hope she remembered to bring my chocolate cherry creams." She started for the door, then turned back. "You're welcome to stay for supper, Pete, although you would do far more good for yourself and others by having supper at the camp."

And with that parting shot, she entered the house, calling for Winnie and leaving Pete behind.

Chapter Seven

Amanda was exhausted. She had a terrific staff, but in the end the responsibility for everything fell to her. When she wasn't worrying about the campers and their progress and safety, she was worried about the bills or the repairs or the need to find yet another grant to see them through some crisis. The latest crisis was the roof on the mess hall. She had thought she could make one more season before replacing it, but a torrential rainfall midweek had made it clear that something had to be done at once.

She pushed her reading glasses onto her forehead and leaned back in the high-backed desk chair her father had used for all the summers he ran the camp.

"I could use a little help here," she said aloud and then practically toppled the chair when she heard a light knock on the screen door.

Boo growled and raced to the door.

"Hey, it's just me, Boo." Pete's voice was gentle and surprisingly welcome, given the fact that she was having trouble thinking about the man without becoming completely unglued.

"Okay to come in?"

"Are you asking Boo or me?"

"Both."

Boo stood at the door, his tail wagging and his paw pushing at the screen.

"Looks like an invitation to come in to me," Amanda said as she stood and made a hasty attempt to straighten her rumpled clothing.

As usual, Pete filled the space he was in. It wasn't that he was so large physically. He was about six feet tall and built more like the swimmer he had been—muscular shoulders and strong upper body, slim hips, and—

"You want coffee? I think there's some left or I could make a fresh pot or—"

Amanda Hunter, what is the matter with you? Stop babbling.

Pete shook his head and looked around the room. She felt as if she could see him recording every detail. But then his focus came back to her.

"I thought maybe we could take a walk."

"A walk?"

He grinned. "Yeah, you know one foot and then the other. Boo could come along."

Now that was just unfair. He knew very well that Boo had understood the word *walk;* the dog started leaping enthusiastically around Pete's feet.

"Did you need to talk about something?"

Pete sighed. "Not specifically, but we might talk. You never know. Or we could just trudge along in uneasy silence."

She took down Boo's leash, which sent the dog into a fresh frenzy of pure joy. "Or you could talk to Boo," she said.

"Not a bad idea." He took the leash from her and let Boo out the door, then held the door open for her.

It was disconcerting to pass close enough to him to be aware of the mixture of soap and the wood smoke from the bonfire at vespers that clung to his skin and clothes. Her shoulder brushed his chest as she passed through the door and the same tingle of awareness she'd experienced with him before shot through her.

As they moved farther away from the lights of the house and into the darkness, that awareness of him walking next to her was heightened. Say something, she commanded herself.

"I hope it doesn't rain for the fireworks," she blurted.

"We need the rain," he replied.

She realized that he was as nervous as she was and stopped trying to force conversation.

"We just had a downpour earlier this week. I have several half-filled buckets that caught the leaks from the dining-hall roof to prove it."

"What were you asking for help with before? Or maybe that should be *who* were you asking?" he asked.

"The mess-hall roof won't make it through the season, but I can't see a way to afford fixing it until the fall. Some of the grants that cover expenses don't come through until after we've demonstrated a successful session. As for who—God or my father or some heavenly force that might be tuned in and able to help."

"You believe in that—I mean, answered prayers?"

"I've seen it work."

"You've also seen it not work, I would think."

She shrugged. "Sometimes the answer is 'not now' or flat out 'no.'"

"And those times when you called for help and none came, didn't that make you angry?"

She thought she knew where this was leading. She didn't want to go there. "Let's get back to the roof," she said.

"Okay." They had come to a fallen tree. Pete took hold of her hand and helped her over it. He did not let go of her hand but continued walking alongside her, his hand wrapped around hers as if it were perfectly normal.

"The roof," he said.

"Needs fixing," she added trying hard to ignore the warmth of his hand enveloping hers.

"And you say there's no money?"

"Not at the moment. At the moment, our only hope is no more rain until September."

"Well, Betsy and Winnie would be against that. They already worry over their gardens if we have a week without rain."

"So there you have it."

"Do you think you might be able to get the supplies donated?"

"Oh, we have the supplies—the shingles and all. It's the labor we can't afford."

"Let the boys do it."

"I couldn't expect the boys to do something like that."

Pete frowned. "I thought your motto was that nothing succeeds like success."

"Yes, but—"

"Well, think of the opportunities for success in this.

For that matter, think of the opportunities for learning new skills, developing self confidence, building teams—"

She pulled her hand free of his and held up her hands in surrender. "All right. You've made your point." She laughed, then realized that it wasn't such a terrible idea.

Pete was more aware of the absence of her hand in his than he had been of the naturalness of holding it. They walked along in silence. He was giving her time to consider his idea and could practically feel her thinking through the pros and cons of letting the boys take on the project.

"Do you know anything about replacing a roof?" she asked after several moments.

"A little, but you don't need me when you've got Dan."

"That's true."

Pete felt disappointment when he would have expected relief. "I mean, I could give Dan a hand."

"That would be nice, but I've really imposed on you enough."

Impose already, he thought.

"Maybe we could divide the roof into sections," she said. "Then we could make each cabin responsible for a section." Her voice rose with excitement.

She was talking to herself, apparently forgetting he was still there.

"I mean, maybe we could line it like a football field, only in feet rather than yards, and, of course, there are two sides so that doubles the space."

"That might work," Pete said, "but if you put this on

a beat-the-clock basis, you're likely to end up with sloppy work and have to do the whole thing over."

"Good point. Still, I really like the idea of a little healthy competition. The boys thrive on that and when it's properly managed—"

"You could have Dan and his crew judge the work, like at each stage—which team cleaned off the old shingles best, which team did the best job on the tarpaper—that sort of thing." He was beginning to come up with ideas of his own. She inspired that—in the kids and in him.

"That's it. They would earn points for work well-done and subtract points for anything that had to be done over or fixed."

He wanted to make this work. "If you like, I could get together with Dan when I'm in town tomorrow and work out the details."

She looked at him as if he had just offered her the moon and stars. "That's wonderful, Pete. I don't know the first thing about the steps involved in roofing, much less roofing a building as large as the mess hall. It would really be a big help."

"Okay." How did she always manage to make him feel so smart and clever and special? "I'll take care of it then," he said, and abruptly changed the subject. "How's that shower working in cabin four these days?"

The day of the Great Roofing Tournament—as it had come to be called—was as promised, sunny and mild, not a cloud in sight. At breakfast the chatter was at a lower level than normal as the inhabitants of each cabin huddled close to their counselors to plan their strategy. Dan and his crew had arrived early to set up ladders and distribute materials and tools around the perimeter of the building.

As Pete approached the podium at the front of the room, Amanda could barely hide her smile. Somehow, following his meeting with Dan, he had ended up in the role of referee. He had even accepted the black-and-white-striped referee's shirt and silver whistle Dan had presented to him that morning. The boys had gotten used to seeing him around the camp. They accepted him. More to the point, he was beginning to accept them.

Led by their counselors, they offered Pete polite applause as he stepped up to the podium. He cleared his throat three times before he spoke.

"Okay, here's the deal," he began. "A team earns points in one way and one way only—safe and precise work. On the other hand, points can be taken away for any number of infractions."

"That's not fair," Antwone shouted.

Pete gave a sharp blast on his whistle. "There's an example now," he said. "Mouthing off to the ref, your coach, even your teammates." He paused and waited for Antwone to slide back into his seat as his teammates scowled at him. "I'd like to thank Antwone for providing us with that example."

"You mean they don't get—" Chad began but stopped when he saw Pete fingering his whistle. "Hey, man, that's great," he ad-libbed, giving Antwone a thumbs-up.

Amanda was impressed with the way Pete had handled the situation. She relaxed and waited for him to continue.

"Other penalties include horseplay, failure to encourage and support other members of your team, foul language and pretty much anything I decide is out of line."

Once again Antwone was half out of his seat, but his teammates restrained him.

"Now, you're all thinking what Antwone so eloquently stated before—'that's not fair.'" He leaned closer to the microphone. "Well, gentlemen, welcome to the real world, where life isn't fair and the only chance you have to beat those odds is to make good choices, find teammates or friends you can trust and give it your personal best."

Amanda scanned the room. Not one boy spoke or shifted restlessly in his seat. Every eye was on Pete. The expressions on their faces had shifted from the suspicion and cocky skepticism of just a few minutes earlier to attentive and impressed. Pete Fleming was a born counselor and coach.

"So Mr. Roark has given you the game plan. There's one more rule—certain safety precautions are already in place. Ignore them and your entire team is out of the competition." He looked around the room before continuing. "If every team does its part, we should have this roof replaced in time to go swimming this afternoon."

Travis's hand shot up.

"Question?"

"Yeah. What does the winning team get?"

"The same thing every man gets when he does his job well—the respect of his teammates, the satisfaction of knowing he did his best and that it was good work, the—"

The campers could not conceal their disappointment. They groaned in unison.

"Oh, you mean like a trophy?"

The campers perked up. He had them once again in

the palm of his hand, hanging on his every word. He grinned, and then pulled out a large trophy from the shelf under the podium. Even Amanda had to be impressed with its size.

"Well, the cabin that wins will have the honor of holding this trophy for the rest of the session and then having it placed here in the dining hall for all future groups to see."

The boys were somewhat impressed, but it was clear they had hoped for more.

"Oh, and Mr. Roark and I were able to get one of the stores in town to donate a new pair of athletic shoes for every member of the winning team—as well as for anyone who receives an individual award." He held up a flashy pair of athletic shoes and every boy in the room cheered.

Hands shot up around the room. "What are the individual awards?"

Pete grinned and waited for the room to become quiet. "Sportsmanship, most valuable player, most assists—and pretty much anything else I decide."

The boys went crazy. They cheered and whistled and pounded the tables and started to chant their cabin number as they closed ranks and filed out to take their positions.

There was no time for Amanda to tell Pete how impressed she was with the way he had put this together and gained the respect of the boys. Dan had appointed her score- and timekeeper and she had her hands full just keeping track of scores and then subtracting points for infractions. By lunchtime, the old roof was off and the base for the new roof was in place. All the boys had to do was put on the new shingles. Dan and his crew would handle the finishing work while the boys went for their swim.

At noon, she watched them file into the dining hall. They were hot, tired and filthy, but she could not remember a time when any session of campers had been more of a community. Aside from the camaraderie that had developed on each team, she now saw evidence of good-natured ribbing across groups. Always with a watchful eye on Pete and his whistle to be sure he was taking note, they called out challenges and compliments to one another. Then as soon as they had their food, they wandered back outside to find a quiet spot where they could form their strategy for the afternoon.

"So pretty tight score," Pete observed and he sounded a little surprised. "I didn't expect them to get into it."

"Are you serious? I would have climbed a ladder and started ripping off shingles with my bare hands after the talk you gave them this morning."

"I just never thought that these kids would buy that 'win one for the Gipper' stuff."

"They're no different from other kids, Pete. They like to win. The trophy and the shoes were strokes of genius."

He grinned. "Actually I need your help on that. See, Dan and I got shoes for all of them so some way every kid is going to have to win something and I'm fresh out of ideas for categories."

His face was streaked with sweat and dirt and his referee's shirt that had been pristine in the morning was in need of a good soaking, but he was smiling down at her with that sheepish grin that had caught her attention the first time she saw it. And those eyes. What had inspired God to give men those lashes that seemed to go on forever?

"Amanda?" His voice was soft, intimate. She caught herself just short of swaying toward him.

"Categories," she said more as a reminder for herself than as a response to him. "Well, we could let each cabin elect its own MVP and sportsmanship winner. And maybe Dan could offer a most promising roofer for each team."

"That's my girl," he said and gave a blast on his whistle as he turned to the others. The boys moved closer to the porch and waited.

"Okay, guys, listen up. Second half coming up. As you can see there's plenty of room for any team to take the trophy. In the meantime…" He went on to explain the voting on each team for various awards and the promising roofer award. Each new idea was met by cheers.

Amanda watched in amazement throughout the afternoon as the boys worked together to complete the roof. She didn't have to subtract a single point. The boys were somewhat self-conscious at first, but soon they were throwing out compliments and high fives as naturally as they had once hurled profanity.

"You're crying," Dottie observed handing her a paper towel.

"I know. Isn't it beautiful, Dottie?"

"The roof? Yeah, I guess if you like green. My personal preference is for red, but then—"

Amanda gave her a light punch on the arm. "You know what I mean. The kids. The way they've all come together."

Dottie grinned. "Yeah. It's something all right." She looked sideways at Amanda. "He's something, as well."

"Dan? Oh, he's the best."

Now it was Dottie's turn to nudge Amanda with her elbow. "We're not discussing that husband of mine and you know it. We are talking about Detective Gorgeous over there. And do not tell me you haven't noticed because you would have to be blind and brain-dead not to notice those shoulders, that chiseled face, that smile, those eyes." She gave a long sigh.

Amanda started to giggle. "Well, I hope Dan doesn't hear you going on like this. I mean Pete's certainly nice-looking—"

"*Nice?* God must have been on quite a roll the day He created that man."

"Dottie, really."

"Really yourself, girl. My understanding is that he's only here for a few more weeks. You'd best make your move—or let him make his, which, by the way, he seems more than ready to do if you would just give the poor guy the slightest encouragement."

Amanda felt heat flame to her cheeks. "Really, Dottie."

"Stop saying that. It's time you got on with your life. Stan—and yes, I am bringing up Stan—would want that for you and you know it. For all we know he sent this gift and, my stars, just look at how he gift-wrapped the package."

"You're drooling," Amanda said and passed her the paper towel as she got up and headed across the compound. "Great job, boys! What a wonderful thing you've done for Camp Good News and for me today. Thank you." She held up her fingers in the signs for "thank you" and "I love you." The boys signed back, "you're welcome."

"Okay, one more surprise. Miss Betsy has invited everyone up to her house tonight for a pizza party and the awards ceremony."

Her voice was drowned out on the cheers at the word *pizza*.

Pete blew a blast on his whistle to quiet them and then bowed to Amanda.

She found she could barely look at him after Dottie's comments. "Thank you," she said turning her attention back to the boys. "Go for your swim and then meet back in your cabins to shower and change. I'll have ballots there for each of you to vote for awards within your team." She performed the sign for "thank you" again, then hugged several of the boys closest to her as they all took off for the lake.

Every window in Betsy's grand old house glowed with welcoming light. In addition, the caterer that Betsy had hired had outdone himself in setting up for the party. The lawn below the patio was lined with tables covered with red-checked cloths and lit with kerosene lanterns. Strings of white Christmas-tree lights wound their way through the trees. The owner of a local pizza parlor had set up shop on the patio where he and his staff stood ready to make pizzas to order. Nearby was another table filled with medals strung on red grosgrain ribbons. Hip-hop music blared from a sound system. Amanda laughed. She wondered how Betsy's other neighbors would handle that.

"Betsy, this is too much," she shouted as the campers and staff eagerly lined up to place their pizza orders.

"Not at all," Betsy replied, also shouting. "Although

the music might be a touch loud. Winnie!" She signaled to Winnie to lower the volume—a move the boys briefly protested.

"I have a few more surprises," Betsy said, her eyes sparkling with excitement. "I don't know when I've had such fun. This roof-raising idea was a stroke of genius, Amanda."

"Actually, it was Pete's idea."

"Really? He's become quite involved with things, hasn't he, dear?"

"It's very generous of him to give the camp so much of his time. I mean, he came here for rest, and—"

"Nonsense. As my Southern grandmother used to say, the man is like a long-tailed cat in a room full of rocking chairs." Betsy paused as if an idea had just occurred to her. "Do you suppose that is the origin of the expression 'nervous as a cat'?"

Amanda recognized it for the rhetorical question that it was and did not attempt an answer. She did hope that the tangent had distracted Betsy from her focus on Pete Fleming, but no such luck.

"The point is, Amanda, that his involvement in the camp and, more to the point, his involvement with you, has done wonders for the boy."

The "boy" was striding up the hill from the boat-house, looking relaxed and fit and ready to enjoy the evening.

"There," Betsy exclaimed, "just look at him. He barely limps anymore—just enough to give him a bit of charm and vulnerability. My stars, if I were forty years younger and that gorgeous specimen had walked into my life—I'd be a married woman today."

"Well, I'll give him one thing," Amanda said, "in the short time he's been here, he's managed to captivate both you and Dottie."

"And Winnie," Betsy added, "not to mention—others." She looked directly at Amanda, then past her. "Hello, Pete, dear."

Amanda turned and found herself looking up into the freshly shaved face of the detective. He wore jeans and a black T-shirt that highlighted his tan.

"Amanda here was just commenting on how wonderful you're looking and how much she looks forward to—"

"Excuse me, please. I see that a few of our young men have left their manners back at camp."

She fled the scene. She was sure that's the way a detective would say it, and it was for certain that this detective had come to that conclusion. After all, his eyes had never left her face, even while Betsy was speaking. Of course, Amanda had known that because she was staring up at him, trying to read his expression as usual. This time she was sure that what she had seen behind that penetrating stare and slightly crooked mouth was a determination not to smile—no, not to laugh.

Was the idea that she might find him moderately interesting so hard to believe? Or was he so used to women falling in love with him that he found the whole thing amusing? Falling in love with him? Where in the world had that come from?

"I am hardly falling in love with anyone, much less someone I've just met," she muttered to Boo as they crossed the lawn to where Antwone and Travis were jockeying for a place in line in front of Chad.

"Go to the end of the line, both of you," Amanda said, keeping her tone firm but without anger.

"Chad was holding my place," Travis protested, his eyes big and round in their mock innocence.

Amanda turned to Chad for confirmation, saw Chad glance nervously at Travis and then the ground. She knew the story here and she wasn't going to have it spoil the evening. "Never mind," she said. "There's plenty for everyone so you two go to the end of the line and wait your turn."

"But…" Antwone protested and then heaved a heavy sigh and trudged to the back of the line.

"Really, Amanda, Travis was here," Chad interrupted. "He—he—had to go to the bathroom, and—"

She placed her hand on Chad's shoulder to stop the string of obvious lies. "This is not about whether you were holding his place, Chad." She looked at Travis. "This is about being a guest in someone's home and being on your best behavior."

"Hey, dude, don't spoil the party," Jake said. "Sorry, Amanda," he added. "They're my responsibility. I got sidetracked. I'll handle it, okay?"

Amanda nodded.

Jake hooked his arm around Travis and pulled him close, grinning at Amanda. "By the way, there's another surprise." He nodded toward the path from the camp.

Mike Connors, the swim counselor, was surrounded by other counselors and staff. He grinned and waved as Amanda hurried down the hill to welcome him.

"Mike! Welcome back! You look fabulous!"

"I do, don't I?" Mike said with mock surprise. Then he hugged Amanda. "It's great to be back. The place looks really terrific and I've been hearing all about this roof-raising thing. What a great idea, Amanda!"

"I really can't take the credit," Amanda said.

"Who's the guy with Betsy?" Mike said.

"That's Pete Fleming. Come meet him," Lexi interrupted as she took Mike's arm and they all started walking up toward the patio. "He's this detective," Lexi continued, eager to tell the story, "and he's been handling the swim sessions with Rob Turner, but he does all sorts of stuff. Like he was the referee today—what a looker. He even cooks, doesn't he, Amanda?"

Yes, the man is a paragon, Amanda thought and wondered if there was a female within twenty miles who was not a member of the Pete Fleming fan club.

"I want to meet this guy," Mike said, quickening the pace. "From what Rob tells me, he's been a big help with the swimming."

After Mike had given Betsy and Winnie big hugs and assured them that he was good as new, Amanda introduced him to Pete.

"Hey, thanks for keeping my job open for me," Mike said.

It was obvious that there was an instant rapport between Mike and Pete. "No problem. You look like you're back in prime condition."

Mike grinned. "Let's just say I came out a lot better than the car did. Rob was telling me that you've been helping one of the kids with his diving."

Again Lexi was there with information. "Chad Devereaux. Weird little guy, but man, can he dive!"

Pete glanced nervously at Amanda. "Well, I may have gone a little overboard with that."

"Oh, no," Mike assured him. "I mean, Amanda has always told us counselors that if we see that a kid can do something well, we need to focus on that. Build self-esteem, right, Amanda?"

Pete's eyebrows shot up and again there was that barely disguised hint of laughter in his eyes.

"It's certainly important to—"

Suddenly the music went dead and Winnie rang a large cowbell. "Ladies and gentlemen," she announced over the microphone, "now that everyone has ordered pizza, please take your places and we'll ask Mike Connors to say grace."

The boys scrambled for a place at the table labeled with their cabin number while Mike took the microphone from Winnie.

"Saved by the bell," Pete said softly as he bowed his head.

"You're faking respect for the prayer to hide the fact that you're laughing at me," Amanda whispered back.

"Children, please," Betsy said as Mike led everyone in the Lord's Prayer.

"Shall we, ladies?" Pete said, offering Amanda and Betsy his arms as soon as the prayer ended.

"Delighted," Betsy said.

Amanda took his other arm without comment.

Chapter Eight

After the main meal, Betsy took the microphone. "Ladies and gentlemen, I believe the time has come for the presentation of our awards. Amanda, would you do the honors?"

Pete led the applause as Amanda stepped to the podium. The boys followed his lead as he stood up and whistled through his teeth in concert with the applause.

Instead of her usual feelings of confusion and embarrassment whenever she was around Pete, she felt only pleasure.

"Thank you," she said, repeatedly signaling for them to stop. "Enough!" But she was laughing and thoroughly enjoying the moment, thoroughly enjoying the way Pete Fleming was looking at her and smiling with genuine admiration.

"Now then, the moment we have all been waiting for," she said, and the group went quiet. "The envelope, please, Dottie."

Dottie handed her a large thick envelope. She took

her time opening it, letting the suspense build. She loved looking down at those upturned faces—so hopeful and filled with boyish excitement. Even Travis Sanders could not hide his hope that his name might be called.

"I'm going to need some help up here," she said. "Since the roof-raising competition was Mr. Fleming's idea, perhaps we should ask him to present the medals?"

The boys leaped to their feet in a fresh round of whistles and applause. Dottie hurried over to Pete's table and pulled him up to the platform.

Pete signaled for quiet. "Please give it up for my beautiful assistant—Vanna Dottie," he exclaimed and spun Dottie around, showing her off.

The younger boys didn't get the joke, but the staff and older counselors did. They led the renewed standing ovation for Dottie.

"We'll begin with individual awards," Amanda announced and once again, silence reigned. "As I call each name, please come forward and receive your award, then return to your table."

The individual awards took some time and once the boys caught on that everyone would receive some award, they relaxed and celebrated each announcement.

"All right, now for the final three awards—most valuable team player overall, most sportsmanlike conduct and, of course, the winning team."

Dottie presented Amanda with three small envelopes.

"The sportsmanship award goes to," she paused dramatically, "Mr. Antwone Richards."

There was a moment of shocked silence and then an explosion of cheers as Antwone made his way through a sea of high fives to the podium. Before he could return to his seat, Amanda caught him and pulled him next to her.

"This is a very important honor because each of you voted for the one other camper who had shown you consideration at any time during the session so far, while the counselors and staff observed conduct during to-day's competition."

Antwone fidgeted and looked as though he'd like to return the medal to get out of this unwelcome spotlight. But Amanda knew the opportunity to teach a valuable lesson when she saw it. She kept her hand firmly on his shoulder. "Antwone received by far the overwhelming number of votes in this category. Antwone, would you like to say a few words?"

Antwone looked at the microphone she held in front of him as if it were a loaded gun. But then he looked out at his audience and everything about him changed. With an athlete's swagger, he took the microphone from her and stepped forward.

"I couldn't have done it without all of you, you know." He began fingering the medal. "Winning is a team effort, you know—of course, without me—you know, like, showing you the way, you would have had big problems."

He shrugged and grinned and everyone laughed. "Seriously, though—you know—I need to thank all the, like, little people—you know who—"

Amanda relieved him of the microphone. "I think— you know—that you've reached your quota of 'you know's' for this victory speech."

Everyone laughed. Antwone grinned and swaggered back to his place where his cabin mates gathered around to inspect his prize.

"Now, for the Most Valuable Player." Amanda tore open the envelope and almost dropped it when she saw the name. She was so surprised that she simply said it. "Travis Sanders."

This time the stunned silence did not end. Every camper either feared or disliked Travis. Every counselor had had to deal with his antics and manipulations and outright defiance. Travis, himself, looked up at her with confusion that quickly reverted to his usual suspicion that he was being tricked.

"While Travis makes his way up here, let me explain that this award was voted on by Mr. Roark and his crew. Dan, perhaps you'd like to say a few words and present Travis with his award?"

Dan nodded and took the medal from Dottie and placed it around Travis's neck. Travis fingered it as if not quite believing it was there. Dan rested his hands on Travis's shoulders and without using the microphone started to speak.

"What's the definition of a valuable team player? Is it the man who scores the most points? Is it the man who takes the most hits so his team can score? Or is it the one person on the team who digs in and does the work?"

He paused. Everyone waited. Travis turned to look up at him, still obviously trying to figure out why he was standing there wearing the Most Valuable Player medal.

"In sports," Dan continued, "it's usually one of those first two—offense or defense—the most valuable is the one out in front, the one with the stats. But in the real world, most valuable defines the guy who shows up, does the work and does it well, doesn't complain, finds ways to do it even better and then goes back and does the same thing all over again."

Dan gave that a minute to sink in. "Today, my crew and I watched every one of you. Travis here was the first on the roof and the last down. He never opened his mouth. He just did the work. He paid attention to instructions, asked questions, did it right the first time. And, when some of you were off moaning and groaning, he finished the work you left undone. That's most valuable in the world where I live. Congratulations, son."

Travis looked as if he'd grown three inches on the spot. His usually slouched posture disappeared as he stood tall and accepted Dan's handshake. And when he turned around, it was Pete who was there to shake his hand. Amanda passed Travis the microphone.

Unlike Antwone, he remained uncomfortable in this spotlight, although it was evident that he was pleased.

"Say a few words," Dottie prodded.

Travis held the microphone too close to his mouth and the system screeched in protest. He lowered it a little and muttered, "I really wanted a pair of those shoes." Then he handed the microphone back to Amanda and hurried from the podium.

Dan and Pete started the applause and soon everyone joined in. Amanda was relieved to see that even though it came late, it was genuine—perhaps as much for Dan's speech as for Travis winning the award—but nevertheless, a moment to treasure.

Thank you, God, she thought as she automatically did at such moments. *Let this be a turning point for him.* She had worried more about Travis Sanders than any other camper that summer. Maybe this would make the difference.

"And now for the final award," she said holding up the last envelope. "The winning team!"

A chant started with cabin one and made the circle until the occupants of every cabin were standing, pounding the tables and shouting their cabin number.

"May I?" Pete stepped forward and she gave him the envelope. He held up his hands for quiet. "And the winning cabin is…"

It was as if all of them were holding their breaths.

"Cabin six," Pete said quietly and the first sounds were Shari and Lexi's shrieks of joy followed in short order by the shouts of their team—the youngest campers.

The older boys from the other cabins applauded, but politely, as Lexi and Shari made their way to the podium to accept the trophy and then motioned for their charges to join them.

"We just couldn't be more surprised or happy," Lexi gushed taking the microphone from Amanda with no prodding. "I mean, this is such a surprise. I mean, we had the littlest kids and we're the only girl counselors and who would think that we could— Thank you *so* much!"

Amanda smiled as she watched the stunned faces of the boys—especially the male counselors from the other cabins who had just been beaten by two girls and a bunch of nine- and ten-year-olds. Behind her, Edna, Grace and Mary had rolled out a covered table. Betsy gave the sign for quiet and it was immediately passed from person to person until order was once again restored.

"And, now," Betsy announced, "I would like to invite everyone to come forward in an orderly fashion and join me for dessert." She signaled the ladies to uncover the table. "Today you built a roof. Earlier you built your own pizza. And now, let's see how good you are at building your own ice-cream sundaes."

On cue, Winnie turned up the volume on the music and the boys lined up to serve themselves. The entire evening was one that Amanda knew she would carry with her forever. She went to find Pete Fleming and thank him.

She didn't have to go far. He was overseeing the distribution of the coveted shoes. Betsy had persuaded the owner of the shoe store to bring out a truckload of shoes in all different sizes. Dottie, Winnie and Dan were busy fitting each kid. Pete was on the sidelines, deep in conversation with Mike and Rob. From their body language, they were discussing swimming. Rob was laughing and gesturing. Amanda had not seen him so relaxed and happy all summer.

She stayed on the fringes, chatting with the campers as they waited to be fitted for new shoes. Finally, Pete stood and shook hands in some ritualistic style with Mike and Rob. When he saw her, he smiled.

"Nice party," he said.

"It's all because of you."

"Hardly. You put it together—you and Betsy."

They walked over to the porch swing in the nook where the front porch on Betsy's house wrapped to the side and sat. As always, being alone with Pete made Amanda nervous. Fortunately, he fixed that when he opened his mouth and said, "Of course, you know this is an aberration. It can't last. Once they go back—" He shook his head and sat forward on the swing, his hands dangling between his knees.

"That's not true. Look at Rob if you need evidence. Why do you have to be so down on them all the time?"

"Experience."

"Well, I've got some experience myself. They *can* change—if you give them the opportunity." She was fighting hard to not be disappointed that apparently nothing had changed for him—even after all that had happened on this incredible day. Pete had simply written these kids off. "I actually thought you had started to come around. I mean, working with Rob and then—"

"Rob is an exception," he interrupted with a dismissive tone that set her teeth on edge. "The rest of them—the vast majority of them—" He left that hanging as he shook his head.

Amanda sucked in her breath and clenched her hands together. "It isn't as if God brought these children into the world with the idea they would end up in jail," she said. Why was he ruining this beautiful day?

"I don't believe there was anything so grand as divine intervention. It was the luck of the draw—I'll give you that—but they came into the world the same as any other kid. From a man and a woman."

"And where are those parents?" she asked, and there was the slightest edge to her voice. "In jail, run off, hooked on alcohol or drugs or worse." She had answered her own question.

"You see, that's where I have a real problem believing in God. If God is so all-powerful and so loving, then how come kids pay the price for the sins of their parents?"

Ah-ha! She had him now. "Don't you see? Bringing a child into the world is a choice we make, and once that child is here, those humans responsible for that child continue to have choices. When they make bad choices, the child pays a price. They are the innocents."

"Look, I know you believe— I know that you are devoted to your—to your faith, but—"

"Oh, stop worrying. I'm not trying to convert you. I'm simply making a point, the same as I would if we were having a political discussion and held different points of view." She took a breath and added. "By the way, I would be right in that case, as well."

She achieved her purpose. She had broken the growing tension between them. He smiled and sat back in the swing, kicking it into motion with one foot.

"Okay, let's stop talking about Rob and talk about Travis."

Amanda sighed. Was he so determined to spoil this lovely day? "What about him?"

"I wouldn't call Travis an innocent." Pete's tone plainly said that this ought to be obvious even to her.

"Oh, but he is. He's making choices based on his limited ability to reason as an adult. He's a child, Pete. They are all children—God's children."

"And please tell me exactly what it is that God is doing to help them?"

She looked up at him and her smile was luminous. "For one thing He sends them here, and for another— at least this summer—He also sent you here."

The swing stopped, but he didn't move or speak. It was a quiet that she was content to prolong.

As the last of the boys got shoes and wandered back to the tables to compare medals and shoes, Amanda stood up.

"I have to go," she said. "Whether you want to take credit for it or not, you made a difference for these kids today. And whether you want to admit it or not, you enjoyed it."

Pete watched her go, watched her stop at each table, say something to the boys, make them laugh or smile before she moved on to the next group. She was a most amazing woman who had been through indescribable loss and yet here she was devoting her life to a bunch of street kids.

He didn't understand that. After the pain she had been through in this place, why did she stay? How could she care about these strangers when her own flesh and blood had been taken from her so suddenly and savagely? How had she gotten past that and moved on?

Maybe Betsy was right. Maybe he could learn something from Amanda about getting through his own trauma. It was for sure he wasn't doing that well on his own. Oh, the days were fine and he even had to admit that the dream didn't come quite as often. The physical exhaustion he drove himself to every day helped with that. But the shooting still haunted him and if he was ever going to get back to being the detective he'd once been, he was going to have to find a way through that.

Amanda was surprised when Pete remained at the party after the shoes had been distributed. She was aware of him talking to Dottie and Dan, then helping Winnie clean up after the caterer left. He even organized some of the older boys to help stack the folding chairs and tables for the caterer to pick up the following morning.

Amanda moved through the group suggesting to senior counselors that it was time to get the boys back to camp and settled for the night. She got no argument and in small groups they headed off to bed.

Once she had thanked Betsy and Winnie again, she called for Boo and headed back through the woods toward her house.

"Amanda?"

When had the sound of his voice calling her name begun to be such an unexpected pleasure?

Boo bounded back to meet him so she could hardly pretend she hadn't heard him.

"Oh, Pete, thanks for everything you did today and tonight. I mean that. It's been a truly wonderful day."

"If you're not too tired, I wondered if we might go for a short walk—or we could just sit down by the pier and talk."

Instinctively, she understood that this was different than other times. He wasn't flirting or challenging her. There was the subtle undercurrent of shyness and reluctance in his voice—as if he wanted badly for her to agree and at the same time hoped she wouldn't. "Is something wrong?" she asked.

"Not really," he replied, but he certainly didn't sound convinced.

"Sure. Let's walk," she said and fell into step with him.

They had walked all the way down to the lakeside path and well past Betsy's property before he said anything.

By that time he had cleared his throat three times in what she realized were all false starts. "Pete, just say it," she said finally.

"Okay. Yeah, maybe that's best." He cleared his

throat again and jammed his hands into the back pockets of his jeans as they walked. "Well, as you no doubt know, something happened back in Chicago—something I'm not ready to talk about yet—but suffice it to say, it's why I was sent here."

"And why you were injured?"

He nodded. "Anyway, Betsy told me a little—that is, just general facts about—uh—about what happened to you, and she seemed to think that maybe if I talked to you, I might learn something."

"Oh, Pete, I don't have any answers. It was Betsy who helped me—counseling me to put one foot in front of the other, to live one hour, one day, one week and then another. And in time and with prayer and the support of good friends, somehow it got a little easier."

"But you still can't really talk about it—even after two years. I mean, the other night when I mentioned your husband—well, it was pretty clear that you didn't want to talk about him or what happened."

"It's hard, and I didn't know you then."

Pete took his time digesting that. "I shouldn't have brought it up now, either, Amanda. I'm sorry. It's a measure of how self-centered I've become that I didn't even think about it from your point of view. Let's just forget—"

She put her finger to his lips, then took his hand and moved toward the water's edge. She motioned for him to sit with her on an abandoned fishing boat.

"Listen," she whispered when he had taken a seat next to her. She closed her eyes.

"I don't hear anything," he whispered back after a minute.

She did not open her eyes. "Of course you do. Just sort it out—the sounds are subtle, but magnificent. Close your eyes and listen."

Pete felt a little silly but he did as she asked. After a moment he became more aware of the gentle lap of the water against the shore, of the call of a night bird in the distance, of the wind passing through the evergreens that lined this part of the shore.

"It was a night just like this when my husband and son drowned," she said quietly, and now he was on full alert.

He didn't say anything for fear she would pull back and not tell him the story. He opened his eyes. Hers were open as well as she gazed out to some distant point in the calm water.

"I would have thought it would be stormy—thunder and flashes of lightning, but no, it was so very peaceful that night." She turned to him. "Do you remember how glorious a day it was that horrible morning when the terrorists attacked Washington and New York? How blue the sky was before the horror? How utterly perfect and ordinary everything seemed?"

Pete nodded.

Once again she studied the water. "That's the way it was the day they died. It had been a really beautiful day that carried into the night. Stars filled the sky as their reflections danced on the water. Danny—our son—begged to take out a canoe with one of the campers he'd become friends with. It was the last night of camp and the boys would have to part the following morning, so Stan and I agreed to let him go."

The light of a passing boat caught her face and Pete

saw tears streaming down her cheeks. The boat passed, thrusting them back in darkness. Pete reached over and took her hand.

"After they'd been out for about an hour, the winds got stronger and clouds rolled in. Stan went down to the pier to call for them to head back. That's when he saw the overturned canoe, but no sign of the boys. He called for me to get help and then started swimming out to them. He found the other boy almost at once. He was clinging to the far side of the canoe, terrified. Stan had to pry his fingers loose."

Pete could not be quiet any longer. "He saved the camper before saving your son?"

"The boy was incoherent and his hold was slipping. He wasn't a good swimmer, and despite camp rules, neither boy had worn a life jacket. By that time others were out there, trying to help."

She paused and Pete recalled how the one time he had seen her anywhere near getting upset with the boys at camp was the day she'd seen Antwone and another boy out in a canoe with no life jackets.

"Stan got him to let go and then turned him over to Dan." She took a long shuddering breath. "And then Stan started to dive—others, too. Everyone tried, but it was night and Danny had been under a long time."

"Where were you?"

"On the shore—watching." A long shuddering sigh. "Praying."

Pete resisted the urge to make the obvious comment that apparently prayer had not worked. That would not only be cruel, it would cause her further pain. At the moment he wanted to do anything he could for her if it would relieve the pain of reliving that horrible night.

"You don't have to tell me this," he said, tucking her hair behind her ear.

She went on as if she hadn't heard. "After a while, the other divers came to shore. They were exhausted, and we all knew the probability of Danny being alive was small. I've lived on this lake my whole life. Like any part of nature, you learn to respect it and know its dangerous side as well as its beauty. We all begged Stan to come in, but he refused."

Pete thought she was going to end it there, but after a long moment, she went on.

"Dan and I took a boat—this boat we're sitting on—it had a little five-horsepower motor then—we took it out to where we'd last seen Stan diving for Danny."

"He was gone?" Pete knew the outcome of the story and figured this was how it had ended.

Now she spoke in almost a monotone. "He surfaced just as we got there—just beyond my reach. 'Come in,' I begged, but he smiled at me. 'I'll be okay,' he said and I realized he was crying, fighting for breath himself. 'I can't just leave him out here,' he said and went under for another search. It turned out to be the last time."

Pete wrapped his arms around her and pulled her close. This was not the romantic embrace he might have fantasized about earlier in the evening. This was something on a much higher plain—the pure and simple need to help another human being through a moment of pain. It had been a long time since Pete had experienced anything like that.

* * *

Amanda stayed there for a long moment, her cheek against the soft cotton fabric of his T-shirt, aware of the rhythmic rise and fall of his chest, like the gentle waves touching the shore, retreating and touching again in an eternal rhythm. She felt his fingers stroking her hair, heard his soft shushing to still her shudders, tasted the salt of her own tears. And, for the first time since that night when her son and her husband had died, she felt a new kind of peace. She had not a doubt in the world that God and Stan and Danny had sent Pete Fleming to her. A perfect stranger who had never known her son or her husband, but who, in hearing the story, had been touched by their loss.

"How did you get through it?" he asked after a long moment.

She pushed a little away so she could look up at him. "Time. Prayer. I know you don't believe in prayer, but it does work and sometimes in the oddest ways."

"Like?"

"Well, like I was watching this television show one night and one of the characters told the other about a quote from the philosopher, Kierkegaard. Something like, one of the most difficult parts of grieving is remembering the future."

"I don't get it."

"Don't you see? That's what I was doing—what we all do. We don't just remember the past when someone dies too soon. We also remember and mourn the future that we planned with or for that person—the future that will never be."

Pete was looking at her, and he had not yet released

his hold on her, although he wasn't restraining her in any way. She realized that he was thinking of kissing her. More to the point, she was shocked to realize that she would not only welcome that kiss, but return it. The idea was stunning—and a little frightening. She stood.

"We should head back," she said in what she hoped was a lighter tone. She whistled for Boo, who emerged from the underbrush with a partially chewed pinecone that he laid at her feet like a prize. Amanda laughed and picked up the pinecone. "Nice try, Boo," she said, "but it's way past our bedtime and we have a full day tomorrow."

Suddenly, she felt self-conscious around Pete. All the way back to the campground, she chattered on, telling him stories of her husband and son designed to make him laugh. He did laugh at some of them, but it was polite laughter at best, and he did not hold up his end of the conversation.

"Well," she said when they reached the edge of Betsy's property. "We were supposed to be talking about you—I mean, that's why you wanted to talk tonight, after all, and—"

Pete cupped her face in his large hands, pulled her forward and kissed her on the forehead. His lips lingered there and when he pulled away, she could still feel the warmth of that kiss. She looked up. His hands still framed her face. She swayed toward him and closed her eyes. "Good night, Amanda," he said and kissed her on each closed eyelid. Then he turned and headed back down the path they had just traveled, only now he was running.

"Okay then," Amanda said to Boo, blinking as she recovered. "I guess that leg of his has really gotten a lot better. Either that or this was just a bit too much sharing for our detective, huh?"

She turned back toward camp and walked with determination to put some distance between Pete and herself—between herself and that kiss. Boo trotted along at her side instead of racing ahead.

"Honestly, I didn't think I had said anything that would cause the man to go running off into the night," she continued as they climbed the hill to her house.

Boo coughed, possibly a bit of the pinecone, but it sounded more like a commentary to Amanda.

"You know, he didn't have to let me tell the whole thing. I mean he actually encouraged it with all that business of holding my hand and keeping quiet and all."

They had reached the foot of the stairs to her porch and Boo cocked his head to one side, then let out a sharp growl before bounding up the stairs and pawing the screen door.

"All right. Keep your shorts on, I'm coming."

Chapter Nine

The scene that greeted her when she opened the door was so unexpected that at first she thought she was imagining it.

The room had been ransacked. Papers from her desk were strewn across the floor. Furniture was overturned. The lampshade was tipped at an angle that left the glare of the lightbulb shining on the now-empty cashbox she kept locked in the desk.

The ramifications of the disaster went well beyond the loss of petty cash and she knew it. Once news of the theft reached the local police and through them, the local newspaper, residents along the lake would be calling for the permanent shutdown of the camp. One core group had been advocating it for years, warning others—especially those new to the area—of the demise of their property values, not to mention their personal safety, if the camp were allowed to continue to cater to these young "hoodlums" from the city.

Without disturbing anything, Amanda walked back

out the front door, down the stairs and across the path to Betsy's.

"Well, my dear, you really have no choice but to report it," Betsy said as they sat in her kitchen sipping tea.

Amanda groaned and buried her face in her hands. Winnie reached over and patted her shoulder.

"Unless—" Betsy said, drawing out the word as both Winnie and Amanda waited for the rest. "That is, in a manner of speaking we have the authorities right here, and since we have little doubt that it was an inside job, then why not handle it internally, so to speak?" She beamed at the brilliance of her logic.

"You mean, ask Pete Fleming to take the case?" Winnie asked and then clapped her hands. "It's the perfect solution."

Amanda thought it not a good time to mention that the last she'd seen of Pete, he'd been racing off, seemingly intent on putting as much distance as possible between the two of them. "That might be an imposition," she said flatly.

"Pshaw," Betsy said. "He works for my nephew. In fact, let's bring Rudy into it, as well. We'll put the fear of God into those little terrors and my guess is the money will be back by noon tomorrow and we'll hear no more of it."

"I can't just let one of them steal and get away with it," Amanda protested.

"Well, of course not, dear. I'm sure Pete will be able to come up with a suitable punishment. Winnie, ring Pete up."

"It's after midnight," Amanda protested, although she could see that it was useless.

"The boy rarely sleeps," Betsy said and motioned for Winnie to dial the old-fashioned rotary-dial phone. As soon as Winnie entered the final number, Betsy motioned for the receiver.

"Ah, Pete! I do hope I haven't awakened you. There's been a crime and we are in need of your expertise. Could you join us here in the kitchen as soon as possible?" She paused to listen. "Absolutely. Take your time. The deed is done. Now on to the investigation with your help." She handed the receiver back to Winnie who replaced it. "Pete needs to dress and then he'll be right here. Winnie, you may want to start another pot of tea while I call Rudy."

The following morning, Pete suggested that Amanda say nothing of the break-in to anyone. Once all the staff and campers had reported for roll call and breakfast, he and Winnie began a search of the cabins.

Amanda and Boo had spent the night at Betsy's. Pete had gone over to her house to secure the crime scene—a phrase that Betsy used repeatedly in her conversation with her nephew. When Pete returned, he called his boss and gave him the details. They had decided that Rudy would drive up to the lake the following morning. They also agreed not to report the theft to the local police—at least for the time being.

The cabin search was a dead end. Nevertheless, Pete had focused his investigation on Travis. Everything he knew about the kid told him he was right.

"No," Amanda said flatly when he told her that he planned to question the boy. "You have no solid evidence to say that Travis is our thief. Either question them all or none of them."

The woman was impossibly naïve when it came to

these boys. "Look—" Pete said, taking care to keep his tone even.

"And that condescending attitude will not help," she said. "I know we need to pursue this. I'm all for it, but unless you have solid evidence that points to a specific suspect, you will question every camper, every counselor and every staff member. Otherwise, I'll handle the matter myself."

Pete looked to Betsy for help, but the doorbell rang and the older woman went to answer it.

"What if you had walked in on them? You could have been hurt," he reasoned and realized that the very idea of that was upsetting on a level of basic and personal caring that he hadn't anticipated.

"What makes you so sure there was more than one?"

"There are signs. They had to be watching the house. They had very little time before they would either be missed at the party or not make it back for bed check."

"Then why all the focus on Travis?" she replied with calm logic. "I mean if you are so certain that there were others—"

Pete swallowed the growl of exasperation he felt rising in his throat, took a deep breath and tried again. "All right. I'll question everyone. It's not a bad idea. One of the others could let something slip. We certainly have nothing to go on at the moment."

Amanda smiled. "I was hoping you would see it my way. I know that the great majority of them had nothing to do with this, but it's so important for them to see that everyone is being treated the same. That we are not assuming anything. That—"

"Amanda, this is a crime investigation, not a camp

learning activity. You were robbed. You could have been hurt. Boo could have been hurt." He was clutching at straws trying to get through to her.

She grinned. "Why, Detective, I think you've started to really care about Mr. Boo."

And you. He almost said it aloud and the surprise of that realization made him even more determined to get to the bottom of this. "Where do you want me to hold the interrogations?"

"Goodness, Pete," Betsy said as she returned to the room with her nephew, Captain Bingle. "Interrogations? That sounds a bit dramatic, don't you think?"

Pete felt color rise to his cheeks. "Captain," he muttered an acknowledgement of the senior officer's presence.

Amanda stepped forward and offered her hand. "Rudy, I'm not sure if you remember me."

Rudy grinned. "How could I forget? You were always making even the older boys at camp look like wimps." He shook her hand and added, "How are you doing? I'm really sorry for your loss."

"Thank you. I'm fine—really."

Pete studied her, looking for any evidence that she was merely being polite, covering her grief. She smiled and continued to make small talk with the captain. He realized that she wasn't just putting on a brave face. She had found some way to deal with her grief and anger— if indeed she had ever felt anger. She had to have been angry on some level.

Whether she had been or not, her tragedy didn't haunt her. She had moved on. He envied her that and at the same time felt a glimmer of hope that maybe time did heal all wounds.

"So, Fleming, what's the plan?" Rudy Bingle was all business as he focused his attention on his detective.

Pete quickly explained Amanda's desire to keep local authorities and the media out of things. Bingle agreed. Then Pete told him his suspicions without actually naming any individual camper. "Amanda thinks questioning everyone makes the most sense. It'll take longer that way, but—"

Again, the sage nod.

"We can conduct the interviews in the camp office," Amanda said. "It's a small room and I think the gooseneck lamp will work well as that light you always see them using in the old movies."

Pete ignored her attempt at lighthearted sarcasm. "The plan is to question them cabin by cabin."

"Staff, too?" Bingle asked, glancing at Amanda for confirmation.

"Absolutely," Amanda said.

"Then let's get to it. Amanda, why don't you get the permanent staff together and let's start with them? We should be able to rule them out fairly quickly. Then we'll take the counselors and, assuming they're clean, we'll have them monitor small groups of the boys while we go through the individual questioning."

"If you don't mind, Captain, I'd like to nose around some more while you question the staff."

Bingle's eyes narrowed. "If you've got somebody you like for this, Fleming, spit it out. Let's not waste everybody's time and put innocent people through undue stress."

Pete glanced at Amanda who said nothing but looked as if she were holding her breath.

"You know how it is, Captain. You always like one or two over the others. I've got nothing concrete."

"Just a feeling?" Bingle asked and Pete nodded. Bingle looked at Amanda and back at Pete. "I've always been able to trust your gut instincts in the past, Detective."

"Well, this is now, sir," Pete replied.

Bingle studied him a second longer and then turned to Amanda. "Well, Mandy, let's go round up that staff of yours."

As the captain had suspected, it took less than an hour to rule out involvement of anyone on Amanda's permanent staff. Just after lunch, Pete started pulling in the senior counselors one by one. He didn't give specifics, just checked and cross-checked alibis for everyone's whereabouts at the time of the "incident," swearing them to silence as each was cleared.

Amanda and the rest of the staff went about business as normal, but she felt edgy and nervous as each counselor exited the office, nodded to her and headed off as if everything were normal. She watched as Rob entered the office. Half an hour later, she realized he was still in there and her heart skipped a beat. Not Rob.

She felt as if she were holding her breath throughout the afternoon. Finally Rob and Pete exited the office together. Rob headed straight for the beach and the afternoon swim session. Pete took his usual position on the sidelines as observer while Rob and Mike ran the session. When it ended an hour later, Pete walked back to the boathouse while Rob and the other boys headed back to their cabins to prepare for supper. She watched for some sign from either Pete or Rob—a smile, a nod—

anything to quiet her fear that Rob was somehow implicated. Neither Rob nor Pete looked her way.

Pete did not come for supper, but just as Amanda was about to start vespers, she saw him head down the hill from Betsy's with Rudy. They were deep in conversation. Both men were dressed in khakis and polo shirts and both men, to her surprise, headed across the campground toward the bonfire.

To her further surprise, when they arrived, Pete began introducing Rudy to some of the counselors and campers, as if the man were his guest. The boys were polite— for the most part—and showed no sign that they suspected anything. The counselors, on the other hand, were edgy.

Finally, Pete and Rudy circled the fire to where Amanda waited. Rudy took her hand between his and said in a low voice. "Now, Amanda, I'm just Miss Bingle's nephew come for a visit. Pete and I are old friends, okay?" Then he added in a normal tone. "It's a real pleasure," and pumped her hand enthusiastically. "Aunt Betsy and Winnie were a little tired and asked that you forgive them."

Pete indicated a nearby log and the two men sat and looked up at Amanda. She began the service. Tomorrow they would question the campers and then everyone would know. She wondered if Camp Good News could ever be the same.

On weeknights, the vesper services were short and ended with the boys heading back to their respective cabins with their counselors to bond and talk through any issues that may have arisen during the day. S'mores were reserved for Friday nights. So as the last strains of Taps died away, the boys left the campfire in silence. Some of the permanent staff members headed back up to the office to finish their daily reports. That left Pete, Rudy and Amanda sitting together staring into the dying embers of the fire. Rudy was the first to break the silence.

"Well, Fleming, seems to me you've got this thing under control. I'll be heading back to the city in the morning. Good night, Amanda. Nice seeing you again."

Amanda stood and hugged him. "Don't be such a stranger," she said. "Betsy misses you."

Rudy chuckled and gave her a mock salute. "Yes, ma'am."

After he left, Amanda busied herself packing up the song sheets and readings she had used for the service. Pete continued to sit, but said nothing. With nothing else to do, she sat down next to him. Boo settled into a curled ball at his feet.

"Well?"

"It was pretty much what we expected," he said.

She waited, but he said no more. "Look, whatever you may think, I would be willing to bet the camp that Rob had nothing to do with this."

As soon as she mentioned Rob's name, Pete looked at her. "I didn't say he did."

Amanda stood and paced. "No. You didn't say anything. You haven't given me any reason at all to understand why you kept that boy in there for the better part of an hour. I thought you suspected Travis and if you think for one minute that Rob would ever help Travis, well—"

Pete was on his feet in an instant. He grasped her shoulders but stopped short of shaking her. His sudden closeness was disturbing, confusing. On the one hand, she wanted to pull away and on the other, she longed to press her cheek to his chest and feel his strong arms tighten around her protectively. What on earth was wrong with her? She needed to focus on the robbery, not being in Pete Fleming's embrace.

"Amanda," Pete said and his voice was gentler than she might have expected. "I need you to trust that I know what I'm doing here."

She looked up and into his troubled eyes. She realized that he was pleading for her confidence in him, that he needed that as much as he needed to solve the robbery.

"I do trust you."

"But?"

"Rob Turner has come so far against such incredible odds. I just can't bear the idea that—" She swallowed around the sudden lump in her throat.

Pete's grip on her shoulders had softened. Now it was more comforting than demanding and the tenderness she felt in that touch was almost her undoing. She brushed away a tear with the back of her hand.

"Hey," he said softly, "it's going to be okay. We'll get to the bottom of this."

"Rob's not involved?"

Pete took a step back. "I didn't say that. All you need to know is that the less you and others know, the less chance our thieves will be tipped off, okay?"

"But—"

"Or I could turn the whole thing over to the local authorities, but my guess is that somebody on the force has an in with a reporter and then—"

"Oh, all right," she interrupted. "Do I get to know your next step in questioning the children?"

"Absolutely. Ask Dottie and the rest of the permanent staff to come up to Betsy's, and I'll lay out the plan."

"I don't think we ought to get Betsy and Winnie any more involved, Pete."

He chuckled. "Well, you'll have to discuss that with them. They seem pretty into this thing and determined to play some part in the investigation."

"Do you think that's wise?"

"I'll train everybody and provide the questions. It's all pretty routine. They'll know what to look for, and then we can go back to anyone whose behavior is suspicious. We can assign Winnie and Betsy to the youngest campers—Shari and Lexi and their group."

Amanda had some doubts but she could find no fault with his plan. "What about you?"

"I'll take Rob's cabin," he said almost as an afterthought.

"Why?"

The look he gave her left no doubt that the subject of why he was focusing on Rob was closed.

"What time do you want to start?"

"Tomorrow morning right after breakfast. You have all groups return to their cabins and we'll question them simultaneously—cuts down on rumors."

She frowned. "The rumor mill is way ahead of you, I'm afraid. They've all noticed the change in routine and the shift in mood."

"Then all the more reason to move quickly. You round up the staff and I'll make copies of the protocol to give them and meet you at Betsy's in half an hour, okay?"

Amanda nodded, but he hadn't waited for her answer. He was already on his way to the camp office to use the photocopier. He moved with purpose and confidence. He was in his element and she couldn't deny that this was *his* area of expertise.

The reason Pete had taken so long in questioning Rob the day before was that he was certain that Rob knew more than he was telling.

"There's been some stuff," Rob had admitted. "I told you—picking on the weaker guys. There's that one guy—well, he makes himself a real easy target."

"Chad Devereaux," Pete had said.

Rob neither confirmed nor denied that, but Pete had been quick enough to see that he was right before the boy's street mask had fallen back into place. Pete tried another tactic.

"Remember the night you came back to camp drunk?"

Rob nodded and watched him warily.

"You said something about an initiation."

"Yeah. So?"

"It just occurred to me that if there's a rite of passage for you as a counselor, maybe there's something similar for the boys in each cabin?"

"I don't know what rites of passage is."

"Initiation. Something a kid has to go through to prove himself."

Rob shrugged, but Pete sensed that he was on the right track. "What I'm thinking here is that maybe the thing at Amanda's place was kind of a trial run for something bigger."

Bingo. The almost imperceptible tightening of Rob's

jaw told Pete he was right. Then again the nonchalant shrug.

"I don't know."

"But what do you think?" Pete asked, leaning closer.

"I think a kid would have to be pretty stupid to try something bigger right now unless he had some kind of a death wish or something." He looked directly at Pete. "I think you've scared off whoever did this."

"And what if I wanted everybody to relax and think we'd found the thief and everything was over?"

That got Rob's attention. "Are you saying you know who did that to Amanda?"

"I think I do, but I've got no proof that would hold up. On the other hand, if the thief—or thieves—thought they could try again—"

"Why would you let them do something like that?"

So it was more than one.

"Because my guess is if I keep pursuing the thing with the cash box, I'll end up with one kid and probably not the ringleader. Somebody will take the fall and my guess is it will be the weakest link."

Rob sat for a long time digesting that. Pete didn't say anything, just let him work it out for himself.

"What if I took the fall?" he asked finally.

Even Pete hadn't been prepared for that. "Why would you do that?" Don't tell me you're part of this, kid— not when I've come to believe in you.

"Well, seems to me that if I did that, then you could maybe get all of them—weak link, ringleader—all of them."

"But if I don't, it's going to be hard for you to prove you didn't do it." Pete checked his notes. "According to this, you don't have any witness for your alibi and there are a couple of others who saw you in the vicinity of Amanda's house when the thing went down."

Rob smiled. "There's a surprise," he said with some sarcasm.

"Meaning?"

"Nothing. You gonna let me help on this or not?"

"Only if you tell me everything you know."

Rob stood up. "Can't do that, man. Are we done here?"

"Look, I'm not asking you to do this for me but you owe Amanda. If we don't stop this now, this whole place is likely to get shut down."

Rob wavered but did not sit down. Pete pressed his point. "You don't have to give me names. Just tell me why you think they plan to hit again."

Rob dug a crumpled piece of paper out of his pocket and handed it to Pete. "I found that. You woulda found it yourself when you searched the cabins if I hadn't found it first."

Pete unfolded the paper, revealing a crude map along with a layout of a house and the surrounding area. "Do you know this place?"

"Yeah. I'm pretty sure it's that great big house at the end of the lake—the one that looks like a castle?"

The Devereaux place. Pete studied the crude drawing and saw that Rob was right. The house Betsy had pointed out had a distinctive tower at one end of the house. To his knowledge, no other place on the lake had such a design.

He folded the map and put it in his pocket. "Thanks, son," he said. "You can go."

"What about my taking the fall? They won't go through with it if they think you're still watching them."

"I don't know." Pete was imagining how Amanda would react to the idea of him allowing Rob to become involved in something that could turn dangerous or could backfire and get the boy sent to jail for something he didn't do.

"I know the place," he said. "All the counselors do— at least we all know the grounds."

Pete waited for more.

"Look, it's a great place to go and hang out on our off time. The old guy never comes out of the house and the place is surrounded by woods and well, some kids use it for one thing and some for another."

"Such as?"

"Hey man, do I have to spell it out for you?"

"Yeah. Spell it out."

"Okay—place to go for making out if you're Shari and Jake. Place to go hang out with the guys. Place to go to write or think if you don't want others thinking you're—"

Pete hid a grin. "Okay. Got it."

"Man, how old are you anyway?"

"Old," Pete replied. "Okay, here's the deal. If I let you take the fall and get involved, we're partners, okay?"

Rob's smile only doubled Pete's concern that he was about to make a terrible decision, but he went on. "Partners *never* go off on their own and I mean never. Partners watch each other's back. Partners stick to the game plan."

After each item that Pete ticked off, Rob nodded vigorously. Well, I've done it, Pete thought and stuck out his hand to shake with his new partner.

Chapter Ten

The following morning, Pete watched the campers from the cabin where Jake was the senior counselor and Rob the junior counselor as they filed in and took their places on their respective bunks. He saw everything from fear to confusion to pure street attitude. Rob was the last to enter the room and did not look at Pete as he passed him and took his place on the edge of a cot at the far end of the cabin.

While Pete didn't think that Rob was involved, he had no doubt that the kid knew more than he was ready to tell. In spite of what Amanda believed about Rob's progress, Pete knew that the hardest thing to abandon was the street code of honor. You did not rat out another kid—even if you didn't like that kid. In the first place, on the streets that kind of thing could get you killed. In the second, even on the streets knowledge was power. If Rob had something on Travis or any other kid, both parties understood that this put Rob in the driver's seat. Pete was counting on that.

Pete closed the door and remained standing with his

back to it, scanning the ten faces in the room without saying anything. Chad met his gaze, then looked down, busying himself with the overlong shoelace of his new athletic shoes. In fact, most of the boys followed that pattern. They probably had had nothing to do with the robbery, but they were well used to being guilty by association. It had not escaped anyone's notice that staff was questioning all the other cabins, but only this one had the attention of the detective.

Pete ended his survey of the room with Travis, who exuded attitude and defiance in the way he had flopped back on his top bunk, turned his back on Pete and started playing a handheld electronic game. Pete walked over and jerked the game out of the boy's hand and tossed it the length of the cabin to Jake.

"Okay, here's the drill," he said.

Travis let out a derisive snort, but when the others did not snicker as he might have expected, he shrugged and gave Pete his grudging attention.

Pete began passing out the question sheets and pencils. "There's been a robbery," he said. "It's an inside job and rather than bring the local police in, Ms. Hunter wants to try and handle it internally."

The room was absolutely still except for the sounds associated with handing out the paper and pencils. "Here's a list of questions. Complete them—sign them. Fold and put them in the bucket at the door as you leave."

"And go where?" Travis asked sarcastically.

"Back to the mess hall. Once everyone is reassembled over there, Ms. Hunter will give you your instructions for the rest of the day." Pete checked his watch. "You have fifteen minutes."

Travis swore under his breath and before Pete could think how to respond, Rob quietly said, "Demerit." Then turned his attention back to completing the questions. Jake nodded in agreement and gave Travis a hard look.

The actual paperwork was unimportant to Pete and, he hoped, to the staff he had trained the evening before. The clues would be in the dynamics. Who glanced around the room? Who cast an intimidating look at another camper? Who finished first? Who finished last?

Pete knew that up and down the row of cabins, the same process was being repeated. He wondered if Amanda would have caught the glance Chad threw Rob and Rob saw, but ignored.

As he had expected, Travis was the first to finish. He sauntered toward the door, taking exaggerated care to fold and refold his paper before dropping it into the bucket at Pete's feet. Then he stood and waited for Pete to step aside and let him pass.

"Mess hall," Pete said.

"I heard you the first time, okay?"

Pete opened the door and watched Travis exit. The boy jammed his fists into the pockets of his jeans and started across the compound. Pete was about to close the door when Jake hastily folded his paper and followed Travis. Travis glanced back at the counselor but kept walking and Jake made no attempt to catch up to him.

Pete stood there a moment observing the two, unsure what he was looking for, but not seeing anything out of the ordinary. He shut the door. He turned to find a line of boys waiting to leave the cabin. Each dropped the completed survey into the bucket on his way out. The last boy to leave was Chad, and Pete's heart sank. The questions had been pretty straightforward—yes or no or one-word answers. If a kid spent time considering his answers, Pete had told the others that was cause for concern.

Pete had begun to think—no, to hope—that Amanda might be right. The camp could make a difference for these kids. For Amanda, the poster boy was Rob. For Pete, it had been Chad. The last boy he wanted involved in this was Chad.

Amanda paced the small confines of the camp office as Pete read through the surveys. He had first read the reports on observations within each cabin from each staff member. His only comment had been, "Nothing unexpected there."

Now he studied the papers from the children, dividing them into piles, occasionally rummaging through a pile to reread a certain child's report.

"Anything?" she asked. She couldn't stand the suspense.

He frowned and laid out three of the papers side by side. "Maybe," was his succinct response. "I need to make a call, and then I'll join you at vespers, okay?"

She was being dismissed. From her own office no less. She left and headed down to the beach to where Dottie and the others had already started the campfire, and the campers were gathered. The tension surrounding that fire was tangible.

Amanda stopped and watched as the campers and counselors went through the routine of setting up for vespers. They were edgy and out of sorts. She heard the sarcasm and angry retorts. She saw the suspicious glances and the intentional shoves.

In just a matter of hours, all the work that they had done to make a difference for these boys—to set them on a better path—had been undone. All that had been achieved in the roofing competition and the party afterward—gone. She was angry and she could not define the direction of that anger. She certainly did not feel very spiritual, but the group was waiting and they needed her leadership. She straightened her shoulders and walked to her place in the circle.

She nodded to Shari, who strummed a hymn on her guitar. As the last strains died away, Amanda watched Pete coming across the compound, watched him circle the perimeter of the group and stop in the shadows. She knew that he had come to observe the group and for reasons she couldn't understand, that upset her even more. She stood and took a deep breath as she looked around the circle at her charges, their heads bowed—not in prayer, but in defeat. Rob was absent from the circle.

"Let us pray," she said quietly and the only sound for the next full minute was the crackling of the fire.

"Our Father," she began and her voice cracked. *"Our Father,"* she repeated with more conviction, *"hear our prayers. We are in pain tonight because the good that we have all worked so hard to create and win for ourselves and for each other has fallen under a cloud of darkness. At this moment, that cloud seems to take up the entire sky and yet in our hearts we know that just beyond that cloud there is light—Your light. We have lost our way as humans often do, but we know that Your love and guiding hand are there in the darkness as in the*

*light. We have only to stretch out our hands and hearts.
We have only to walk in truth and that truth will lead us
out of the darkness and into the light. Help us to understand that even though the path to the light may seem
more dangerous than simply staying in shadow, it is the
only way. Amen."*

She nodded to Shari, who played a second hymn.
During the music, she saw that Pete was watching her,
not the campers. She could not read his expression, but
there was no question that his eyes were on her. When
the hymn ended, she stood again.

"This has been a very difficult couple of days for all
of us. But it has been especially hard for those involved
in the event under investigation. You know who you
are. We want you to know that you are in our hearts and
prayers, that we know you are in pain and that you are
suffering. How do I know this? Because I know you—
each of you. And what I know is that children do not
have the capacity for evil. In your lives you have each
gone astray. But I believe that in your hearts, you want
to do good. Each of you has that potential to do good in
your lives, in the lives of others. We will get past this.
Those involved will have the chance to apologize, make
amends and seek forgiveness, and we will move on."

She paused and looked around the circle. Everyone
was looking at her now, and in their eyes she saw a desire to take hope and comfort from what she was saying. They wanted things to get back to normal as much
as she did. Only a few looked at her with cynical eyes.
"I give you my word," she said.

She nodded to Shari who played Taps. At the last note
when the boys would have automatically dispersed, she

held up her hands in a gesture of benediction. "Go in peace. Go in love for your brother who may be suffering. Tomorrow is a new day—let us be glad and rejoice in it."

She signed "I love you," and one by one others around the circle repeated the sign.

Pete's initial gut reaction to Amanda's service was pure skepticism. Then the boys filed past him on their way to their cabins and for perhaps the first time since becoming involved in the activities of the camp, he saw them for the children they were. He saw them as Amanda saw them—boys who had lost their way or fallen through the cracks of the adult world. He watched as two boys passed him, their heads down, their steps dragging, and then the older boy reached over and put his arm around the shoulder of his younger companion. And in that simple gesture, Pete understood that these boys weren't even different from the so-called "good" kids. They had just drawn the short straw of life.

But a crime was a crime and someone would have to pay.

He was trying to decide the best way to break the news to Amanda when Boo came bounding up to him, tail wagging, and planted both paws on his leg. Amanda sat alone watching the fire burn itself out.

"Okay, boy," Pete said to the dog. "No time like the present." For her own safety, he had to make her believe it was over. With the dog at his side, he went to Amanda.

"Well?" she asked, not taking her eyes off the fire.

"You're not going to like it."

"Just tell me."

"I'm afraid Rob won't be here for the rest of the session."

"I will never believe that Rob had anything to do with this and there's nothing you can say that will make me accept that."

"Look, Amanda, I just can't tell you everything. You're going to have to trust that I'm a little more of an expert in things like this than you are."

"Rob doesn't have a motive," she argued.

He'd known that she would fight him, but he was ready for her questions. "Maybe not. On the other hand, we know that Rob's mom has cancer and she might benefit from a new expensive medicine. What's missing is just a drop in the bucket for what it would cost, but kids don't look at it that way. All they think about is the money."

Amanda turned to him, her features beautiful, but tragic in the dying firelight. "Rob would never have vandalized my home."

Pete shrugged. "Amanda, these kids carry all sorts of stuff that they keep under wraps until sometimes it just breaks through. Every one of them, including Rob Turner, has every reason to be angry at the hand he's been dealt."

"That doesn't explain the damage."

Her questions unnerved him. He hated what this was doing to her. He wanted it over.

"I can't explain that for sure. My best guess is that the money wasn't as easy to grab as they thought. With time running out, they got desperate. Things got turned over and broken."

She looked at him for a long time, forcing him to meet her gaze. "You're not telling me the truth," she said.

He didn't even try to deny it. "I'm telling you what I can, Amanda. This is a police matter. I'm doing what I think is best for everyone involved—including you," he said. "I need you to trust me. I promise you it will be all right in the end."

She started to say more, but didn't. He would have given anything to find some way to take away the pain she was going through, but he knew touching her, holding her would be the wrong thing now. If his plan worked, this would be over in a few days and he could explain everything.

"What about the others?" she asked after a long moment. "You said 'they,' so it was more than one."

"I thought it had to be Travis and that he'd gotten Chad involved somehow. But Jake grudgingly provided alibis for both boys and Shari backed him up."

"Shari's head over heels in love with Jake. She'd say anything he told her to say."

Pete nodded. "I considered that, but it fits the pattern of the robbery. They all have alibis for the time of the crime."

"So where was Rob? Because he was not robbing my house."

"On the way back from the party, he told Jake that he needed to talk to you about something. Maybe he intended to tell you about his Mom, to get help and then—"

"Just stop it," Amanda said angrily. "Stop it." The words did not come in a shout but in a guttural growl just before her voice broke. "What does Rob say?"

"He says that he did stop by your house because he

thought he saw somebody in the window. When he got there, he saw the overturned furniture, the open cash box, knew someone had robbed you, and panicked."

"Well, there you have it."

"Not really. The stories don't match, and Jake has backup. Rob doesn't."

She looked up at him. "Pete, I don't know how I know this but I do. Rob Turner is protecting someone. He's too smart not to realize that he's the prime suspect, and if it were true and he knew that, then he would have run. He hasn't left the campgrounds since this happened." He could see she was looking for straws she could clutch at. "If the money was so important, then why hasn't he tried to leave and get it to his mother?"

"Amanda! It's over. I'm doing the best I can to make this turn out right, okay?"

She opened her mouth twice to say something and then shut it. She wrapped her arms around her knees and rocked herself. "So now what?" Her voice was barely a whisper and yet it rang with defeat.

"Rob's going back to Chicago tonight."

Amanda stood up. "Does he know?"

"He knows."

"Aren't you afraid he's run by now?"

He hated the sarcasm in her tone, hated that his actions had caused that. "Look, I'm sorry. I'd give anything if—"

She took a long breath before speaking. "No, *I'm* sorry. You're just doing your job. It's not the outcome I wanted, but that's not your fault." She kicked sand into the last glowing embers. "I'll go help him get his stuff together. What time will they be here to get him?"

"I thought I would take him back if that's okay with you. It might be easier on him."

"Thank you." He saw that she meant it.

"Why don't you bring him over to the boathouse when you're ready? We'll leave in an hour."

She turned and seemed unable to decide what to say or do. Finally she stuck out her hand for him to shake. "Thank you again, Pete."

He bypassed her outstretched hand and pulled her into his arms. "I know you don't believe this," he said softly, his mouth close to her ear, "but Rob's going to be all right. I give you my word." He held her a minute longer and then released her and walked toward the boathouse.

"Are you coming back?" she called, and it was as if he'd waited forever to hear those words.

Fighting a lump in his throat, he nodded without turning back or breaking stride. "I'll be here for the fireworks," he called to her when he found his voice.

Rob had already packed when she reached the cabin. He sat alone on his bunk, stuffing the last of his clothes inside his duffel. The other boys were in their bunks pretending to be asleep. Rob's new athletic shoes were lined up next to the bunk. Amanda picked them up.

"You forgot to pack these," she said softly.

"Didn't forget," Rob murmured without looking up. "They're yours."

He shrugged. His hand trembled as he pulled the zipper on the bag closed.

"Rob?"

"I don't wanna talk about it, okay?"

She hated that he wouldn't look at her. Somehow she had to get through to him. She pulled him into the bathroom and shut the door. She spoke in a low tone meant for his ears.

"Rob? I don't know what's going on with you. What I do know is that *if*, and that is absolutely an *if*, you had anything to do with the robbery, you thought you had a good reason and you didn't mean to do damage or hurt me or anything like that."

Rob stared at the floor.

"You always believed in me," he said quietly.

She grabbed him and hugged him hard. "Oh, Rob, I will always believe in you—no matter how many times you may take these wrong turns, I know that in the end you will find your way. And when you do, I'm going to be there just as I am now, okay?"

He nodded and pulled away. "I got to go," he mumbled and opened the door, grabbed his bag and headed outside.

"I'll walk you to the boathouse. Pete's going to drive you back." She picked up the shoes and followed him. "I'm sure there's still room in that bag for these."

He hesitated. She remembered how thrilled he'd been with the shoes.

"Go on," Amanda said. "Maybe they'll help you figure out where you belong."

Rob took the shoes and stuffed them inside the bag. "If you think I did this thing, how come you're not mad?" he asked.

"I'm sad and hurt to think that you might have had anything to do with this—that anybody here had something to do with this. That doesn't mean I stop trying to help you."

Huge tears coursed down Rob's cheeks. Amanda held out her arms to him and he walked into the circle of love and forgiveness that she offered.

"I hate thinking I've hurt you," he said, his voice choked with sobs. "I wish—"

"Shhh. We'll get through this. We'll find some way to get through this." She held him a moment longer, then gently urged him forward. "Come on. Pete is waiting."

After Pete and Rob had left, Amanda was restless. She tried to work and ended up walking through the camp. It was different. She no longer felt that aura of innocence that had always come at night when the children were sleeping. Tonight she and Boo walked through the camp checking outbuildings and jumping at the slightest noise. It was as if they were looking for problems, and she hated that.

It was hardly the first time there had been trouble in the camp. There had been other thefts. There had been fights. There had been runaways. She knew the risks of trying to make a difference in the lives of troubled boys. The disappointment she felt in Rob Turner came with the territory.

Then why does it feel so different?

Is it because I'm afraid that Pete Fleming is right about the boys—about Rob?

Was that it? "That's ridiculous," she said aloud and Boo looked up at her and wagged his tail in confirmation. "Come on, Boo. Looks like Betsy is still up and that means the kettle's on." A talk with Betsy Bingle had always restored Amanda's sense of well-being.

"Winnie is staying the night with her sister in Milwaukee," Betsy reported as she led the way to the den she had always favored over the more expansive living room. "Poor dear had a fall and Winnie was worried, so I told her to go and see for herself." She curled herself into an overstuffed, chintz-covered chair and cradled her teacup with both hands, blowing on the steaming liquid as she watched Amanda.

Amanda took her usual place on the sofa, kicking off her shoes and sitting cross-legged. Boo made three circles and then settled into his customary spot on the hooked rug in front of Betsy's chair.

"Well?" Betsy said after their small talk had faltered and silence had taken over.

"I didn't want it to be Rob," Amanda said.

"Yes, I know, dear. And yet I think your coming here tonight may not be as much about Rob as you would like to think."

Amanda frowned. "Who else would it be about?" And she knew the answer before the words were out of her mouth.

"This is about Pete Fleming, dear. This has been about Pete almost from the moment the two of you met."

"He's so cynical—especially when it comes to the boys. I really wanted him to see the difference we could make, and—"

"Have you considered why it should matter to you one way or another how he views the boys?"

"Because—that is I—"

Betsy reached over and patted Amanda's knee. "It's because you care what he thinks of *you*."

"Oh, for goodness' sake, Betsy. I know you've been hoping for a romance, but really—"

"I don't deny that. But this isn't about a foolish old

woman's wishful thinking. Amanda, dear, for the first time since Stan and Danny died, you have come alive this summer, and I could not be happier—or more relieved."

"Betsy, I am no different—it's just time healing me. It has absolutely nothing to do with Pete." She had pushed away the memory of the feel of his lips that night before she discovered the robbery, but could not seem to forget the feel of his strong arms embracing her earlier. On both occasions she had felt the stirring of something she had been so certain had drowned with Stan and Danny.

"It seems to me that you've finally seen another person who is in as much pain as you were," Betsy said as if Amanda had not spoken. "Pete's suffering, like yours, is tied to an event in his life over which he had no control and one that came seemingly from nowhere."

They sipped their tea.

"He kissed me," Amanda whispered, not fully realizing she had spoken aloud.

Betsy waited for her to continue and, when she didn't, continued for her, "And you felt something reawakening inside."

"There was nothing romantic about it," Amanda assured Betsy and herself. "It was a simple peck on the forehead." Not exactly. His warm lips had lingered. She had felt his heart beat against her palm, and the way he had cupped her face with his hands and then kissed her again on each tear-stained eyelid.

"Ah," Betsy said knowingly as she refilled their mugs. "Answered prayers."

"Really, Betsy, I hardly think that someone as obviously burdened with his own troubles as Pete Fleming is—"

Betsy raised one finger to silence her. "That's it. All along I've been thinking that God sent Pete to help you, but it's quite the opposite. It's you who are to help Pete. Have you considered the idea that you may be God's answer to Pete's prayer—to *his* cry for help?"

"Pete doesn't believe in prayer or God for that matter."

Betsy smiled. "That rarely gets in the way of God going about His business." She set down her mug and reached over to take Amanda's hand in hers. "Open your heart, dear girl, and let God do His work for both of you."

Amanda clung to the thin but surprisingly strong hand of her friend and mentor. Then she sighed. "And what of Rob? How did I miss that? I thought he had come so far."

"And you were right. He has traveled a great distance. He has further to go. And the good news is that he now has both you and Pete to go the rest of the way with him."

"I just can't believe it was Rob," Amanda said softly.

"That's because you know there is more to the story. That is what you and Pete will uncover once he returns. He is coming back, isn't he?"

In that moment, Amanda felt the weight of the events of the last several days grow lighter. Pete had said he would return. "For the fireworks," she told Betsy.

Betsy laughed and stood. "Well, I wouldn't expect anything else. He definitely strikes me as a fireworks sort of guy," she said with a wink.

"Why Betsy Bingle!" Amanda tried to sound shocked, but Betsy's wide grin made her smile and then laugh out loud. Boo woke with a start.

"Time to go, Boo." Amanda linked arms with Betsy as they walked through the house to the back door. "Thank you," she said and kissed the older woman's cheek.

"My pleasure, my dear. Try and have a little faith in God's plan and in Pete and yourself as instruments of that plan."

Amanda had her doubts about how Pete might see himself as God's instrument. The thought made her smile and that night she slept soundly for the first time in days.

Pete watched the captain study Rob Turner. For his part, Rob met the captain's eyes without defiance.

"You sure about this, son? Taking the rap for somebody else?"

"Yes, sir."

"It could backfire on you. Right now you're all we've got—everything points to you. You'll go away—maybe for a long time—and definitely for something you didn't do."

Rob glanced at Pete. "It won't backfire, sir. The detective here has it all worked out."

Rudy Bingle shifted his gaze to Pete. Now it was Pete's turn to straighten in the hard wooden chair and meet the intense scrutiny of his captain.

Pete could almost guess what he was thinking. What if something happens to the kid? Déjà vu all over again.

"It's not the same as last time," Pete said, and took satisfaction in the slight expression of surprise that crossed the captain's face. "I walked into that blind. This time I'm—we're—calling the shots. We've got a chance to nail the Joker, Captain."

"You think Joker is behind this?"

"I think he's right there in camp."

The captain rubbed his chin as he considered that, then turned back to Rob.

"Who else is in on this?"

"No one, sir," Rob replied.

Again Rudy looked at Pete. "What about Amanda?"

"She doesn't suspect anything." *I hate deceiving her like this. Hate having her think she's failed with Rob.*

"And my aunt?"

Pete shook his head. "Look, Captain, if this thing goes down right, we can keep it all within the confines of the camp. If you veto the idea, then there's going to be a break-in that will flash through that community like a wildfire and it will shut the camp down for good. I don't think you want that."

"I know I wouldn't want that, sir," Rob added. "Ms. Hunter and Miss Bingle have made all the difference for me and my mom. Miss Bingle getting her the medicine was like a gift from heaven—that's what Mama called it. Called her a servant of God."

Pete smothered a smile as the boy began to sound more and more like a storefront preacher selling his case.

"All right," Rudy Bingle said abruptly.

"Sorry, sir," Rob mumbled and resumed his customary stoic silence.

Rudy turned his attention to Pete. "You'll take Kalazinski for backup."

"That's not—"

"Detective, that was not a question. You will take your partner back with you for backup, understood?"

"Yes, sir," he replied.

Pete could see that Rob was mesmerized by the way the pudgy, rumpled man behind the desk was ordering Pete Fleming around. The teen seemed even more fascinated with the way Pete accepted the order without argument or defiance. "So go through this thing again for me. When do you think it'll go down?"

Rob and Pete pulled their chairs closer to the Captain's desk, and Rob took the lead in laying out what they knew and the plan they had come up with to thwart the robbery.

Chapter Eleven

Chad Devereaux had been acting strangely all week. Amanda suspected that it might be tied to Pete's absence. But without Pete there as a buffer, she noticed other things. Like the way he avoided Travis Sanders. In spite of his surprising performance at the roofing competition, Travis was a bully. Most of the campers could handle him, but he had targeted Chad now that Pete wasn't around to protect him. The odd thing was that Chad had not transferred his obvious need for protection to Jake or one of the other counselors.

"Chad, I haven't seen you practicing your diving this week," she said as she slid in next to him just as the boys were finishing supper. "You know, now that Mike's here, he could work with you. He's an excellent diver himself and besides teaching swimming, I'm sure he would be more than happy to—"

"I'm sorry, Amanda," Jake said, breaking off his conversation with Antwone and leaning forward. "I've got Chad here and the other boys all working overtime on the surprise for tomorrow night before the fireworks."

Chad nodded enthusiastically, but there was something in his eyes. Amanda had embraced Jake's suggestion that the boys in cabin four put together a special Fourth of July skit. The activity had taken everyone's mind off the empty bunk where Rob used to sleep. The boys seemed full of ideas for a special patriotic performance to entertain the rest of the camp as they waited for dark and the fireworks display across the lake. Jake had even managed to get Travis involved.

"We're all very curious about what you have planned," Amanda said.

"Well, the one thing I can tell you is that Chad is due for a costume fitting up at Miss Bingle's, right, dude?"

Chad nodded, gathered his dishes and hurried from the table.

"Is he all right?" Amanda asked.

"Devereaux?" Jake shrugged. "You know how it is, Amanda. They get attached. He liked Rob and, of course, he was getting pretty tight with Fleming. I think he might be having some trouble working on loyalty issues—like, is it okay to still like Fleming, who busted his buddy?"

It made sense and Amanda recognized elements of her own teaching in his words. She patted Jake on the shoulder. "Well, thanks for coming up with the idea for tomorrow night. Maybe it'll help."

Later, as she and Boo walked past the cabin on their nightly rounds, she heard the boys practicing patriotic songs. Their youthful voices strained to reach the impossibly high notes of the "Star Spangled Banner" and she had to smile when she heard them collapse in giggles as someone's voice cracked.

"Come on, Boo," she called and took off running

along the path. All day her energy had been high. Tomorrow, Pete would be back.

Tomorrow. Tomorrow. Her feet pounded out the rhythm of the word and her heart grew lighter with each step. And, in that moment she admitted to herself that whatever the future might bring, Pete Fleming had broken through the wall she had built so carefully to prevent an opening for any hint of personal need or desire. She felt free—free to let go of the pain while holding the good of the past in her heart forever. She ran with joy and a lightness of spirit she had almost forgotten. By the time she stopped running, she was well past Betsy's property. In fact, she was on the narrow, encumbered path that crossed the property belonging to Chad Devereaux's grandfather.

She stopped to catch her breath and looked up at the somber dark mansion and thought of the bitter old man who was a legend in the community. Over the years, going all the way back to her father's time, he had led the fight to shut down Camp Good News. She recalled all the times that she and Stan had tangled with the man at various civic meetings, how many times they had taken valuable time from the campers to address some trumped-up petition backed by Walter Devereaux.

How different might Chad's life have been if he had been surrounded by the kind of warmth and love that flowed from a home such as she'd known, or even that of Betsy Bingle? Instead, he had grown up with bitterness and a certain festering anger passed down from his grandfather to his father and now to him. Was that what Pete had meant when he said Chad reminded him of himself as a boy? Had he too endured a father's disapproval?

She saw a single light glowing in a downstairs window and actually considered trespassing across the manicured lawn littered with "No Trespassing" signs to have a talk with the old man himself. Surely a grandfather, she thought.

Then the light went out, and Amanda knew that any opportunity she might have had was gone. She whistled for Boo, who had ignored the signs and was sniffing at something under one of the immaculately trimmed bushes that lined the property.

"Come on," she said softly. Boo trotted along beside her as she retraced her steps. She started out walking but picked up the pace to a light jog as the path became more defined and in no time was crossing Betsy's property and winding her way around the boathouse back to the compound.

Another light caught her attention. A light in the loft of the boathouse. Her heart raced. Was he back? She ran up the steps to the deck and peered through the sliding doors. But the shades were closed and she could see nothing. She looked up again and saw no light. She walked around to the other side of the house. No car. Concerned, she tiptoed up to the door and tried the handle.

The house was locked tight. She walked all around the house looking for any signs of an intruder. Everything seemed fine. Then she noticed the way the light of a passing houseboat reflected briefly on the kitchen window and then disappeared. That had to be it. Remembering the glimpse of light, it had seemed too dull to be a lamp even behind closed shades. And, on reflection, it had wavered. It must have been a passing boat.

"Tomorrow," she murmured to Boo who gave a low woof of agreement as they both headed for home.

Pete could not seem to keep the loopy grin from his lips as he watched Amanda lead the pack of campers down to the beach just after supper. He had gotten back just in time to change and make an appearance at the celebration. He would meet up with Jud and Rob later.

It was important that everything seem as normal as possible. The last thing they could afford at this point was to tip off the real thieves. In a few hours it would all be over. He just hoped that Amanda would forgive him for the subterfuge.

So he stood on the deck watching Amanda Hunter, dressed in denim bibbed overalls over a white T-shirt and wearing a ridiculous Dr. Seuss red-white-and-blue-striped top hat, leading the campers and their counselors to the beach. Boo brought up the rear, wearing a patriotic T-shirt of his own. The sound system from the mess hall blared out march music, and Pete could not help noticing that hard as they tried not to, the campers had fallen into step and were marching along in time to the music.

"Pete!"

Pete turned around and saw Winnie and Betsy coming across the lawn via a golf cart that had been decorated for the occasion. "Come on. We'll give you a ride."

Pete hurried to join them, glad that he had had the good sense to choose a red T-shirt to wear with his jeans instead of the black one he usually favored. As he climbed into the cart, Betsy presented him with a denim baseball cap emblazoned with the words *God Bless America.*

"It completes the outfit," she said with a satisfied smile. "Amanda will be pleased."

Pete put aside all thoughts of how the day was likely to end and concentrated on enjoying the festivities. He had already spotted the main suspects in the parade of campers. As long as they were in sight, he could afford to enjoy the day.

When they reached the beach, he helped Edna, Mary and Grace serve up a picnic feast of hot dogs, potato salad and apple pie with ice cream. And all the while he watched Amanda. He was sure she had seen him, but she was obviously avoiding him by focusing on managing the old-fashioned games she and the rest of the staff had set up for the campers.

"Sack race," she called holding up two burlap sacks. "Somebody has to get this going. Shari?" Shari held up a just-filled plate and shook her head.

"I'll do it," Pete called out. "If you'll race against me." He pulled off his apron and held out his hand for one of the sacks. Immediately the campers surrounded them, cheering and chanting for Amanda to compete.

He could see that she was thinking about Rob. Her eyes were alive with unasked questions.

"He's fine," Pete assured her in a voice meant for her ears alone. Then in a louder voice, he demanded, "Well?"

"I'm the referee," she protested.

"Not a problem, dear," Betsy said. "Anyone who can blow a whistle can referee." She motioned for the whistle.

Pete saw Amanda look around for some other excuse and finding none, she grinned and gave up one of the sacks, keeping the other for herself.

"I'm very good at this," she warned him as they each stepped into a sack and hopped to the starting line. "Do you want a head start?"

"No, thanks. But I would like to make things more interesting."

"On your mark," Betsy shouted.

"No bets, Detective," Amanda replied with a stern wag of her finger. She waited for Betsy's signal.

"Get set!"

"How about a prize," Pete replied, hitching his own sack higher. "If I win, you'll buy me dinner. If I lose— which is unlikely—I'll buy, okay?"

Amanda blinked. Pete grinned. He had caught her completely off guard. Betsy blew the starting whistle and Pete took off leaving Amanda standing at the starting line.

The campers and counselors lined the route, cheering and chanting as Pete breezed toward the finish line. And then out of the blue, there she was, taking unbelievably large leaps as she caught up to him.

"Okay to dinner, but you cook," she yelled as she hopped past him.

Desperate to save face, Pete doubled over and groaned. He kept the sack clutched in his one hand as he rubbed his leg with the other. It worked.

In a split second she was kneeling next to him, her face a portrait of genuine worry. Her own sack was puddled around her ankles, forgotten in her concern for him.

"Are you hurt? Your leg—is it? Oh, this was stupid. I completely forgot about your injury. I'm so sorry."

He motioned for her to come closer, grimacing in pain as he did so. "You are so easy to fool," he whispered and then straightened up and hopped the final two steps to the finish line. The campers loved it, and Pete took full advantage of his victory, striding around accepting high fives and pumping his fists victoriously in the air.

Betsy blew several sharp blasts on the whistle. "We need a ruling," she called and Pete looked at her in disbelief.

"What are you? The NFL? I won. Fair and square."

"You may have crossed the finish line ahead of your opponent, Pete, but the rest is in question. I believe this can be settled with another contest."

Pete and Amanda both gave her a skeptical look. Betsy was unmoved. "It seems to me that rather than beating one another, the true lesson you wish to impart on this day of our nation's birth is that of the value of working together. Therefore, I propose the tried-and-true three-legged race through an obstacle course. Jake, dear, please do the honors."

Jake took a length of rope and tied Pete's ankle to Amanda's with a nautical knot he'd been showing off to the other campers a week earlier. In the meantime, Betsy directed other campers in setting up the course.

"I don't get it," Travis argued.

"The point, dear boy, is that if these two can successfully work with, instead of against, each other and traverse the course without mishap in sixty seconds, then it will be my pleasure to host an outing to the movies this coming Saturday."

The campers needed no further incentive. Suddenly they were as invested in the outcome of this race against the clock as they had been when the race pitted one per-

son against another. They took their places along the
route and called out advice about how best to negotiate
each obstacle and beat the clock.

"Put your arm around her waist," Antwone ordered.
"She won't bite."

Pete did as he was told and then Antwone gave
Amanda an exasperated look. "Well?"

Amanda snaked her arm through Pete's and felt him
tighten his grip so they were literally joined at the hip.

"Ready? Set. Go!" Betsy called and gave a blast on
the whistle.

They came close to toppling twice, but each time they
righted themselves and moved on. Halfway through the
course, they developed a stride that seemed as natural
as walking alone. The minute it happened Amanda
looked up at Pete and he grinned. "That's my girl."

As soon as they crossed the finish line, the children
surrounded them. Even after the rope had been removed, he kept his arm around Amanda as the boys
whooped victoriously.

"All right," Amanda shouted above the din and held
up her hands. But she was laughing and Pete could see
that she was enjoying the moment as much as he was.
He also thought that she had never been more beautiful. And with a clarity he hadn't known in weeks, he realized that he was in love with her.

They were enjoying their hot dogs when she told
him about the light in the boathouse. Jake had taken several of the campers off to prepare for their performance
and the others were feasting on the leftovers from the

picnic and listening to Betsy's stories of celebrations on the lake when she was a girl.

"I thought you had gotten back last night," Amanda said after he had once again assured her that Rob was all right and that he would fill her in on all the details after the fireworks.

"I would have stopped by if I'd gotten in last night." He scanned the crowd gathered on the shore. "Where are Travis and Chad?" he asked nonchalantly, but she heard in his tone that he suspected something.

She laughed. "They're in the skit Jake has put together. Relax." He certainly seemed tense for someone who kept assuring her that everything was all right.

"Anyway," she continued, "I took Boo for a run, and on the way back I thought I saw a light up in the loft. But then I checked and your car wasn't there and—"

He had stopped listening when she'd said where she'd seen the light. "In the loft?"

"I'm sure it was just the reflection of a passing boat."

"What time was this?"

"Around eleven. Why?"

Suddenly Pete was on his feet and moving toward the boathouse. "Look, I forgot that I have to check on something for the captain. A detail we forgot in making the case. Nothing for you to worry about. I might miss the fireworks, but if it's okay, I'd like to stop by later."

She stood, as well. "What's going on? What are you keeping from me?"

Just then one of the boys came running down the path from the cabins to say that they were ready to start the performance. The boy pushed Amanda's top hat

into her hands and a script for announcing the per-
formers. Pete seized the opportunity to head for the
boathouse.

Amanda tried to concentrate on the camper's instructions for introducing each performer in concert with
the recorded music, but her thoughts were with Pete.
She watched him say something to Betsy and Winnie
and then take off for the boathouse at a run. She sent the
camper off to get Dottie to act as her stand-in and followed Pete. By the time she reached the boathouse, she
could hear him upstairs in the loft.

Pete ran up the spiral staircase to the loft, but it was
fear, not exertion that lay behind his shortness of breath.

You never should have left your weapon behind.

He opened the closet and felt along the top shelf.

Please, let it be there.

It was gone. His gun was not there.

There was a time when that gun was as much a part
of your everyday routine as strapping on your wrist-
watch. What's with you, man?

He dragged a bench over and stood on it to be sure,
and his heart sank. The unloaded gun was not the only
thing missing. The bullets he'd packed in a small tin box
were also gone.

He hated this business. What had these kids been
thinking? One of them was on his way to the Devereaux
place with a loaded weapon, and—

"Pete?" Amanda's gentle voice did little to calm his
panic. She was standing at the top of the staircase. He
hadn't heard her come in. He had heard only the sound
of his own blood racing through his head as he tried to

think what he could do to stop the tragedy that might already be beyond his control.

"I have to go," he said. All he could think about was that the plan was in motion and he needed to warn Rob and Jud.

She blocked his way to the narrow stairway. Short of physically lifting her aside, there was no way he could squeeze past her. "Amanda, get out of the way," he said.

"Not until you tell me what's going on. When you said you'd be back for the fireworks, you weren't talking about the Fourth of July, were you? Something is going on—something upsetting."

"I'll explain later. Right now, if I don't get— If you don't get out of the way—"

"I'm coming with you. You can explain on the way." She turned and ran back down the stairs. "Well, come on."

He didn't have time to argue with her. "If you're coming then you have to do exactly what I say, when I say it and there can be no questioning that."

She nodded and he saw that her eyes must mirror the panic and fear she read in his. "Can you at least tell me who's involved?"

"Right now it looks like Travis and Chad. Rob may be walking into a trap, not to mention my partner, Jud Kalazinski." He grabbed his keys from the kitchen counter. "If you know a shortcut to the Devereaux place, now would be a good time to show it to me."

He had the engine started and the car in gear before she had closed the door. "Take that turn," she said tersely when they reached the main road. He made a sharp left onto a rutted gravel road so narrow that the branches of the trees whipped at the sides of the car.

She said nothing. Instead she leaned forward, peering into the gathering darkness, looking for landmarks and not asking him why he refused to turn on the headlights. "Here," she said. "This will take us to the back of the house."

"How far?"

"Maybe half a mile."

He pulled the car to a stop. "We'll have to walk."

Still she did not ask questions. "There's a footpath," she said keeping her voice low. She pointed to a place he really couldn't see and he noticed her hand shook. She was scared and he was the cause.

"Amanda, wait." He reached for her hand and held it between his own. Her fingers were ice-cold even though the night was hot and humid.

"Did Rob escape?" she asked, her voice shaking, as well.

Pete put his arms around her and held her. "Okay, here's the *Reader's Digest* version. Rob was never the suspect. He found out the real thieves were planning to hit the Devereaux place, but had backed off when we started the investigation at the camp. It looked like Travis Sanders was our ringleader in camp and I thought the strings were being pulled by his gang leader from outside—a guy called Joker. Somehow Travis was able to bully Chad and Antwone into working with him, and now I'm pretty sure the Joker's in camp."

"Not Rob…."

"Rob overheard a couple of things and I took it from there. He agreed to take the fall for the cashbox so the real thieves would think they had a clear field to go ahead with the robbery tonight as planned. Rob and my partner are staked out there and judging from what I saw at the campfire just now, Travis and the others are on their way."

"And the Joker?"

"Back at camp establishing his alibi."

"But something's gone terribly wrong."

He took a deep breath and held her tighter. "Yeah. Somebody has my gun."

"Travis?"

"Or the Joker. My guess is that Chad took it for him."

"Oh, Pete, we have to stop them—stop this madness." She pulled away and hurried along the path. He had no choice but to follow her, and as close as they were to the house there was no chance of further conversation.

He caught up to her, stopping her before she broke free of the cover of the woods and ran out onto the lawn. He motioned toward a single light on the first floor.

She mouthed the word *library*.

Pete nodded and took the lead. He motioned her to stay put and worked his way up to the window. Inside, he saw an old man dozing in a high-backed leather chair. Then he saw a shadow run past the pocket doors of the room, followed by another. The boys were inside the house.

Pete looked around and saw Antwone huddled in the brush next to the back door of the house. Knowing Antwone had not seen him, he returned to the cover of the woods. Amanda wasn't there, but before he could look for her, his pager vibrated.

Pete clicked it on. The message said that Jud and Rob were in place and ready to go. Pete sent back the message that one of the kids had his gun. At first there was no response, then a terse: Roger that. Let's roll.

Afraid that Amanda had decided to take matters into her own hands, Pete ran across the lawn to the house. The plan was for Rob to handle Antwone while Pete and Jud went inside. Like someone born to undercover work, Rob called out to Antwone and got him away from the house by telling him he'd broken out of jail and needed help. Eager to fill Rob in, Antwone abandoned his post, and Jud and Pete were inside the house in seconds.

They could hear the boys rummaging around upstairs. Pete approached the back stairway. "You go find the old man and let him know what's going on," Pete whispered. "I'll handle this." He pointed up the stairs.

Jud nodded, then pulled his own service revolver out and handed it to Pete. Pete's hand shook slightly as he took it. "This is different from that night," Jud said, reading his partner's mind. "It's just different, okay?"

Pete nodded, and Jud moved soundlessly down the corridor toward the front of the house. Pete climbed the stairs and moved down the wide hallway toward an open door.

"You'd better not be trying to pull a fast one here, Devereaux," Travis hissed as Pete took up his position just outside the door.

Chad's voice was choked with fear. "I'm not. I know the combination, but you have to be exact or it won't open."

"You'd better hope you're right, man. Otherwise we're both dead. You heard what he said."

"I heard him. I heard him say this was it—after this no more. I passed my test when I took the cash from Amanda's. After this, he's gone, you're gone and we're done."

"For somebody who's gone to all them fancy schools, you are one dumb rich boy," Travis drawled and Pete could imagine the scornful smile.

"I mean it, man. This is it. I get you the cash. We leave. Grandpa doesn't find anything missing until next time he comes to the safe and by that time—"

He was quoting what had obviously been drilled into him as the plan. No doubt he had repeated it over and over to himself until it had become a mantra. Pete actually felt sorry for the kid.

Travis snorted. "You just keep on believing that, rich boy. You are dumber than dirt, dude."

Pete heard the safe click and at the same time the squeak of the bed as Travis leaped into action. "Oh, man!"

"Just take the money and let's get out," Chad begged.

A few seconds later, Pete heard the safe click closed, the sound of the painting that covered it sliding back into place, hands smoothing the covers and then the boys ran right past him and headed for the stairs, carrying a pillowcase stuffed with money.

Amanda had been so focused on watching Pete that she hadn't heard a thing. Then more suddenly than she would have believed possible, a hand was covering her mouth and she felt what had to be the barrel of a gun pressed to her temple.

Half a dozen options leaped to mind, none of them viable. She thought of biting the hand, but any sudden action might cause her attacker to pull the trigger. She thought of the self-defense training Stan had insisted she take when they took over the running of the camp. Noth-

ing she had learned there had prepared her for a moment
like this. She saw Pete start back across the lawn and
let out a small squeak meant to warn him.

"Move," her attacker growled and pushed her ahead
of him back down the path toward a small clearing.
There, he pushed her to the ground and then fell heavily on top of her. Her face was pressed into the wet
grass and she could hardly breathe, much less warn
Pete.

Don't let him get hurt, she prayed, and, sensing her
best bet for protecting Pete was to lie docilely beneath
the man with the gun, she forced herself to relax.

After what seemed an eternity, the man leaned close
to her ear and whispered, "Well, there goes lover boy. He
sure didn't spend much time looking for you. I guess his
cop job is more important to him than you are. Get up."

He stood up and waited for Amanda to push herself
to her knees, then held out his hand. "Come on,
Amanda. Move. I don't have all night."

She looked up and into the smiling face of Jake Buntrock. He was obviously delighted with her shock. "I told
you I had a few surprises planned for tonight," he said
and jerked her to her feet. "I'll admit I hadn't quite
played it out this way, but a little insurance never hurts.
Now, just stay put until we get the signal."

The gun was now pressed to the small of her back as
Jake held her in front of him and watched the house.
There was no sign of Pete or his partner or of Rob.
Could they be out there, watching, waiting? Perhaps if
she could keep Jake talking.

"Jake, I don't know what this is all about, but—"

"What this is about is my getting enough money to

blow this place and never look back—never have to see you or these ghetto kids or little old ladies who think they're so smart or my so-called father—" His voice broke a little.

"I'm sure we can work something out, Jake. It's not worth any amount of money to have to spend the rest of your life on the run, is it?"

Jake laughed but there wasn't a hint of mirth in the sound. "You know what you are, Amanda? You're one of those people who need to think that there's some good in everyone. That's what you've preached at the camp day in and day out and you have no idea how many of us are laughing at you behind your back."

"Your laughter is just a mask for your fear, Jake."

"Yeah, well, you keep on telling yourself that, sweetheart. One of these days you're gonna wake up and smell the coffee. You think we like coming to your stupid little camp, pretending like we're buying into the vespers and the team spirit and the—"

"Camp Good News has saved many boys just like you, Jake. It's not too late."

"Lady, you're as batty as that old lady Bingle. You sit here on your fancy lake, pretending to lead the simple life when all along you have everything you need—you never once in your whole life had to struggle for anything, did you?"

Amanda could not hold her tongue a minute longer. "Jake Buntrock, you are hardly the one to talk about being deprived." She knew immediately that she had gone too far. He turned on her and his eyes blazed with fury.

"You don't know the first thing about my life. Just because there was plenty of money and stuff—" His voice cracked with emotion and she thought he might break down. "There's other kinds of want than *stuff*. You can't begin to know, so just keep that mouth shut for once."

She would not give up on him. "I know that God loves you, Jake. I know that you can find peace and forgiveness if you stop now. Let me help you."

"Peace? Really? How come your oh-so-perfect God lets kids like me end up with parents who decide that sending me to an inner city school instead of letting me go where my friends are, will make me a better person? Well, the laugh's on them. I put together my own gang—it was the only chance I had. And now I'm buying my freedom on the Fourth of July. What do you think of that?"

They had reached the back of the house. The door was open. Jake seemed momentarily confused. He paused and looked around.

"Antwone," he called in a whisper.

When there was no answer he grabbed Amanda again and pressed the gun to her temple, pushing her up the back stairs ahead of him.

"Keep quiet," he ordered, "or I swear that I will pull this trigger."

Amanda forced herself to think of good things for she knew it was the only way to defeat the fear that threatened to overcome her. She thought of the loving home she had known as a child. She thought of the maternal friendship Betsy had provided after her own parents had died.

She thought of Stan and the years they had spent building the programs she knew worked at the camp.

She thought of her little boy, Danny, and for the first time in a long time, she remembered him playing soccer and laughing at Boo's puppy antics rather than that horrible night when the divers had carried his limp and lifeless body from the lake.

Finally, she thought of Pete and knew without a doubt that God had brought him into her life to help her get to this new place, accepting the past and moving toward a new future. Now she was going to have to fight for her chance at that future.

"Jake, I believe in you and I'm praying for you," she whispered. "Whatever happens here tonight, I forgive you."

She felt the gun relax ever so slightly, and then press harder against her head. Jake stopped abruptly and waited.

Amanda heard the deep reassuring rumble of Pete's voice on the stairway above her.

Chapter Twelve

Pete let Chad and Travis get a third of the way down the stairs and then stepped forward, Jud's gun still at his side. "Hello, boys." Travis and Chad froze in their tracks. "What's in the pillowcase?"

Travis tightened his grip on the pillowcase. Chad looked as if he couldn't decide whether to be terrified or relieved.

"Why don't we all go downstairs and talk this out?"

The boys walked down the wide stairway like prisoners headed for the chair. Pete saw no evidence of a gun, which confused him. Surely, they hadn't entrusted the gun to Antwone.

Jud and Walter Devereaux stood waiting for them at the entrance to the library. Pete honestly thought Chad was going to throw up as his grandfather stood there without a word, his silence more punishing than any reprimand.

"Thank you, detectives. I can handle this from here," Devereaux said as soon as the boys were inside the library.

"No, sir, I'm afraid it's not that simple," Jud replied.

Devereaux frowned. He was a man used to giving orders, not taking them, no matter how gently they might be given.

"Officer—"

"Actually, sir, we're detectives," Pete said, "and these young men are in more trouble than you know." He turned to the boys sitting side-by-side on the leather sofa. Travis was working hard to maintain his tough-guy facade. Chad had abandoned all pretence and was sobbing uncontrollably.

"You see, sir, one of these boys has a gun—my gun—stolen earlier from the house where I'm staying."

Both boys looked up at him and in that instant, he knew that neither of them had taken the gun or had it on his person.

"Hey man, I'll cop to burglary, but I got no gun," Travis blurted.

Pete turned his attention to Chad. "Any ideas?"

Chad's eyes widened and he seemed focused on something behind them. Pete whirled around and saw Jake standing in the doorway with a gun—his gun—to Amanda's head.

"Joker," Chad whispered.

"I should have known better than to trust you," Jake snarled at Travis.

"Jake, please—" Amanda said softly.

Jake pressed the gun barrel to her forehead. "Shut up for one time—just shut up." The camp clown was deadly serious and dangerously angry.

Pete fingered the gun he'd managed to conceal at his side. He took stock of everyone's position. Travis and

Chad remained on the sofa, their eyes wide with fear and panic. Jud stood behind the sofa and reached over to place a comforting hand on each boy's shoulder.

That's it, partner, keep them calm, Pete thought.

Walter Devereaux had resumed his place behind his massive desk just before Jake had made his entrance. Now, the old man was slowly opening a desk drawer and Pete could see the glint of a gun barrel inside the drawer.

No, old man, do not go for it! He glanced at Jud and then back to Devereaux. Thank heaven for years of working together. Jud read his signal.

"Now, let's all just calm down here," Jud said quietly as he moved away from the boys and toward the old man.

"Stay where you are," Jake shouted.

Jud held up his hands and at the same time used his knee to close the open desk drawer. "Look, son, you don't want to hurt anybody. Let's just all—"

"I'm calling the shots here," Jake shouted. The room went quiet as he glanced wildly around.

"Pick up the pillowcase, sweetheart," he ordered. Amanda did as she was ordered, her eyes never leaving Pete's face. She seemed to be trying to tell him something. Then he saw that she was signing the words *I love you,* and in that instant he knew that she thought this would be her only chance to tell him that.

"Hey, man," Travis said, "I ain't taking the rap for no shooting. The money is one thing but—"

"Shut up!" Jake screamed, waving the gun at each of them. "Just everybody shut up! Let me think!"

For a split second the gun had been removed from Amanda's head, but immediately it was back. Jake forced her farther into the hallway.

"Everybody outside. Now!"

Pete and Jud nodded to Walter Devereaux and the two boys. "Just stay calm. Do what he says," Jud instructed them.

Pete used the distraction of everyone moving toward the door to tuck Jud's gun into his waistband at the center of his back. As the two of them passed Jake, Jud positioned himself to screen Pete so Jake wouldn't see the weapon.

Once they were outside, Jake looked around, deciding his next move. Then he smiled. Pete saw that his gaze was focused on the pier where a small fishing boat rocked gently in the water.

"Down there," he ordered.

Where was Rob? Pete looked around quickly as they joined in the forced march to the pier.

Just as they reached the pier, Walter Devereaux stumbled, but Jake only tightened his hold on Amanda. "Sit, old man!" He nodded toward a lawn chair. Then he turned his attention to Chad. "Crybaby, make yourself useful. Start the motor and keep it idling. We're going for a ride." He started walking backward down the pier, dragging Amanda along with him.

Pete saw movement in the shadows of the neighboring property. Rob and Antwone were working their way down to the water's edge. Antwone stopped, but Rob slipped into the water and started swimming toward the fishing punt.

Jake was almost to the boat. "Get in," he ordered Amanda. She glanced back at Pete. Slowly he reached for his weapon. There would be one second when Jake released her into the boat that he would have a clear shot.

Amanda hesitated and Jake slapped her hard with the back of his hand, then grabbed her by the hair and pushed her off the pier and into the boat. Pete raised his gun.

"Drop it, Jake. It's over. Let her go and drop your gun and we'll see what we can do for you." He moved toward them along the pier.

Jake pointed the gun at Amanda, holding it steady with both hands. "I'll kill her, man. Right here and now. I'll kill her."

"You shoot her and I shoot you—everybody loses," Pete said, fighting to keep the rage he was feeling out of his voice.

"Don't do it, Joker," Travis begged. "Please, let her go. She never did nothing but good. Let's just take the money and get out of here."

Jake laughed. "You're as stupid as your name, Cockroach. *We* aren't going anywhere—just me and her and the crybaby—they're my insurance. See, the old man there will protect his own and my old man will see that nothing happens to me—not because he cares, you understand. No, he'll be really ticked about the whole business, but he'll come through because what if the precious Buntrock name makes the news in a bad way?"

He paused, lost in thought, and Pete moved a step closer.

Jake grinned, focusing his attention on Chad. "And then I met this guy, and I thought to myself 'Jake, how much better to embarrass *two* of the big-shot families— the old-money-and-therefore-we-are-entitled families on the lake." He shifted his gaze to Walter Devereaux and there was pure loathing in the look.

"Jake?" Amanda said softly.

He glanced at her briefly and then turned his attention back to Pete. "Her future's in your hands, Detective. Either way I win."

"How do you figure that, Jake?" Pete asked, buying time.

"My life's pretty much a wash either way. I shoot her—you shoot me or I don't and you don't, and she's my ticket out of here. Either way I get what I want out of this whole business."

Pete lowered his gun slightly, and Jake laughed. "Let's go," he growled at Chad and prepared to jump into the boat.

Everything happened in a matter of seconds, but it played out in slow motion for Pete. Amanda had sat up, nursing her split lip with the back of her hand. As Jake started to jump into the boat, she reached up and grabbed his leg, throwing him off balance. Jake kicked her hard.

At the same instant that Pete raised his gun, Travis streaked in front of him and headed straight for Jake.

"I said don't hurt her!" Travis screamed.

Just then Rob reached the ladder to the pier. Jake waved the gun wildly. It went off just as Travis tackled him and Rob fell back into the water. The gun went flying.

Pete and Jud ran for them, but Jake had already knocked the smaller Travis off the pier and he was ready to leap into the boat when Chad suddenly revved the small motor and pulled away. Jake stepped off the pier and into the water, and Jud jumped in after him.

In the silence that followed, Pete's first thought was of Amanda. He waded out to the boat. "You okay, kid?" he asked Chad as he reached over and cut the motor.

Chad nodded.

Pete turned to Amanda who reached for him with both arms.

"You're bleeding," he said brushing back her hair.

"It's nothing," she said as she searched his face for any sign that he had been hurt.

He couldn't stop touching her face, her hands, her hair. "I'm so sorry, Amanda. I never should have let you come here. You could have—"

"Shhh." She pressed her fingers to his mouth and smiled. "You know better than to think you could have kept me away."

He smiled and turned back to Chad. "Hand me that rope and let's get you both back to the pier."

On shore, Jud had dragged Jake from the water, handcuffed him and was reading him his rights. Pete glanced around, looking for Rob, Travis and Antwone. His heart beat faster. It was quiet—too quiet.

Suddenly Antwone emerged from under the pier. "I need some help here. Rob's been shot."

It was impossible to say whether it was Pete or Amanda who reached the wounded boy first. Pete got him to shore, where he lay on the dew-soaked grass, not moving. Chad tied up the boat and then went to his grandfather. Antwone hovered around Rob. Travis was nowhere to be found. In the distance, fireworks exploded in the clear sky. Just like that other night, Pete thought. That night when the kid died.

Amanda was kneeling next to Rob, cradling his head. She looked up at Pete, but he didn't see Amanda. He saw that other boy's mother. He saw that mother's eyes accusing him as she held her already dead son.

Pete flinched as Jud came up beside him. "Ambulance on the way," he said to Amanda as he put his arm around Pete's shoulders. "The Sanders kid must have made a run for it."

Pete nodded but barely heard his partner. He couldn't take his eyes off Rob's inert body.

Not again! He prayed and in that instant realized that it *was* a prayer—a plea for some force greater than himself, greater than any weapon, to step in and make this right. *Please. If You're up there, don't let—* He felt hot tears plop onto the backs of his clenched fists. *Please!* He couldn't begin to form any more coherent words.

Rob moaned and tried to sit up.

Thank you, Pete thought.

Amanda cradled Rob, whispering words of comfort as he lay there, moaning softly. From what she could tell, the bullet had hit him in the shoulder.

"Lie still," she urged. "Help is coming. Listen. I hear the sirens. Just lie still."

She gently stroked his forehead and looked up at Pete. "He's all right," she said, but realized Pete was not hearing her. He was staring at Rob as if he were seeing someone else.

"Pete, he's okay," she repeated and still he stared blankly at the boy. "Pete!"

Just then they heard a cry for help from the water.

"It's Travis," Chad said and headed for the end of the pier. "He's in trouble."

"Not a good swimmer," Rob managed.

Amanda looked up at Pete. "Detective!" she said sharply.

Pete blinked and seemed to see her clearly for the first time since they'd pulled Rob from the water.

"Probably thought he could swim for it," Rob said, grimacing as he tried to sit up. "Can't tell that kid anything."

They heard a splash.

"Chad!" Walter Devereaux cried and rose half out of his chair.

Pete ran the length of the pier and dove into the water. When he surfaced, Amanda could see Travis flailing about before going under. Chad was several lengths from him, but swimming with confidence and strength.

The paramedics had arrived and she turned Rob over to them while she went down to the edge of the pier and watched—as helpless as she had been that summer night two years earlier.

Travis surfaced briefly just as Chad reached him and then went under and did not resurface. Pete had seen him as well, but was still too far away. Chad dove. Amanda's heart slammed against her chest wall as if she were running a marathon.

She saw Chad surface, grab air and dive again. Pete reached the place where he'd gone under and dove in. Amanda could only imagine the blackness beneath the surface. Would the explosion of fireworks help at all?

She ran to the boat. Every movement seemed a replay of the night her husband and son had drowned, but she would not think of that. She had to get to them. She ripped the cord to start the motor and blessedly, it caught.

The surface of the water was placid as she maneuvered the small boat to what she thought was the right spot. Then suddenly she saw them. First Chad sprang to the surface and gasped for air. In the next instant, he dragged Travis above water as well, and then Pete was there with them. They were safe. She turned the boat and ran it as fast as the small motor would allow.

She helped drag Travis over the side, then Pete boosted Chad into the boat before climbing in himself. As soon as they reached the pier, Pete pulled Travis out of the boat and called for the paramedics. Meanwhile Chad helped Amanda secure the boat and climb onto the pier.

Amanda wrapped her arms around Chad, who was shivering badly, probably from shock. "You were wonderful," she assured him repeatedly. A paramedic tossed her a blanket and she wrapped it around Chad.

"He thought he could get away," Chad told her through chattering teeth, "but he's not that good in the water. He was really scared."

"But you saved him, Chad. That was very courageous."

"Yes, son, you did the honorable thing," Walter Devereaux said. He had come down to the pier as soon as Chad dove into the water. Now he held out his arms to his grandson and when Chad went to him, Amanda went to check on Travis.

Pete was pacing back and forth, first questioning the paramedics about Rob's condition, then checking on Travis and Chad, then taking a call on the cell phone Jud handed him.

"It's the captain," Amanda heard Jud say. Pete nodded and walked away from everyone while he took the call.

Amanda sat down next to Travis, rubbing his thin shoulders through the blanket. "That wasn't very smart, Travis," she said gently. "If it hadn't been for Chad—"

"Yeah," Travis replied and his voice reflected his surprise. "I mean, who woulda thought—"

"He's a very good diver and he's spent a lot of summers swimming in this lake."

"Not that stuff. Why would he care whether I drowned or not? Why did he do it?"

"Wouldn't you have done the same for him? Didn't you try to do the same for me?"

Travis looked at her and swatted at the tears that suddenly overflowed. "Jake made it sound like this was gonna be easy. He never said nothing about no gun— or hurting you—"

"Still, you knew it was wrong," Amanda reminded him.

"He was in charge," Travis said as if that explained everything.

"Oh, Travis, are you going to spend your whole life letting others take charge for you?"

Just then Chad joined them. "You don't understand, Amanda. The Joker is really slick." He sat on the other side of Travis, not touching him, but there was no question that he wasn't going to abandon him. "He came after me and I didn't even know it. Got me caught up in that trouble that got me sent here and that was just the start of it. If it hadn't been for Rob…"

"You got that right," Antwone added as he stationed himself behind the other two. "It's like Rob told me. That dude uses guys like us to do his dirty work."

"And we let him," Travis added. "Like Amanda says, we had choices." All three boys nodded glumly.

Amanda saw Pete flip the phone closed and hand it back to Jud. He glanced her way briefly, but instead of coming to her, he walked back up to the house.

"You boys stay here and do whatever the officers or paramedics ask of you, all right? I'll be right back."

"I'll see that they do," Walter Devereaux assured her.

"He said he was going to the hospital," Jud told her when she couldn't find Pete anywhere on the estate. "It might be good to give him a little time, ma'am. There was another—"

"I know about the other shooting, Detective, but this is not the same thing at all."

"Maybe not for you or me, but for Pete—well, it's another kid shot on his watch. Another kid shot with his gun. That kind of thing will eat at you if you let it. Pete's likely to let it."

"Not as long as I'm around," Amanda said more to herself than to him. "Do you have everything under control here?"

"Got it covered, ma'am. The Turner kid is on his way to the hospital. I'll get the perp back to Chicago. Meanwhile, those three look pretty shook up. I don't expect they'll try anything more tonight. They can wait until tomorrow."

"All right. Thank you."

As she left the house, she heard Walter Devereaux insisting to the local police who had arrived on the scene with the ambulance that his grandson be remanded to his custody.

"And Travis and Antwone, too," Chad said with surprising force. "I'm not staying here without them."

"Then you'll go to jail," his grandfather replied.

"Then I will," Chad shot back.

"Very well," Devereaux said and his voice showed

his exhaustion as he turned to Jud. "If it suits you, detective, the three boys will spend the night here. I'll take full responsibility."

Jud took the local police aside to explain the arrangements. Amanda started to leave, then turned back to Walter Devereaux. He looked frail and every bit as frightened as the boys. She went to him and took his hand in both of hers. "It's going to be all right, sir. They are good boys at heart. They just need someone to believe in them."

"We'll discuss that at a later time, Ms. Hunter." Devereaux gave her a piercing look that left no doubt that he had not changed his opinion of the camp.

She turned her attention to the three boys. "You will *not* disappoint me any further tonight, is that understood?"

"Yes, ma'am."

"I suggest that you use the time you have here to think about the choices you have made these last few days and the consequences of those choices. We'll talk tomorrow."

"Yes, ma'am." Their heads were bowed and they looked much smaller than their years. Her heart went out to them. "Come here," she said softly and the three of them moved into her open arms. When she broke the embrace, all three of them were crying and as she walked away she saw that Walter Devereaux was watching the boys with interest. There was no doubt that he had the attention of all three boys, and there would be no further problems. At the same time, Amanda was relieved to see the way the old man rested one hand protectively on his grandson's shoulder.

* * *

The car was gone so she took the path. As she approached Betsy's property, she saw the lights in the boathouse. The car was parked next to the house and the trunk was open. Just as she approached the sliding doors, Pete came out. He was carrying a duffel bag.

"Where are you going?"

He tossed the duffel into the trunk and slammed the lid. "Back to the city." He wasn't looking at her. She recognized the signs. He was deliberately shutting himself off the way she had for the weeks and months following Stan's and Danny's deaths.

"Rob is going to be fine."

Nothing.

"Don't you care?" It was a hurtful thing to say and she knew it, but she had to get through to him. He turned on her, his face ravaged with pain, and she would have given anything to be able to take that pain away.

"Of course, I care. What kind of monster do you think I am?" His words came out in an angry staccato spray.

She reached for him, but he backed away, warding her off with upturned palms.

"It wasn't your fault, Pete," she said. "It's not like the other time. You know that. Listen to me—" She grabbed his arm, but he shook her off and got in the car.

"You can't make this right, Amanda, so don't try." He started the engine, and softened slightly. "Look, I've got some stuff to figure out."

"I thought that's why you came here to the lake," she said without reproach.

"Yeah. Well, things just got more complicated. It's better if I go back to the city—better for everybody," he added before she could say anything more. Then he pulled away before she could do anything to stop him.

Just as he drove off, the finale of the fireworks began. She could hear the campers shouting their delight at the show. And then a blaze of light shot into the sky, lit the area like daylight, and then slowly faded and fell into the black water, and the show was over. She stood on the deck watching the last ember die. Her head was spinning with the chaos of the last hour. "Rob!" she said aloud, realizing that she needed to get to the hospital.

She caught up with the rest of the camp staff as they left the fireworks, and she told them what had happened and what they needed to do to manage things for the rest of the night while she was at the hospital. As she drove to the hospital, she called Betsy and filled her in on the evening's events.

"He left," she said when Betsy kept asking about Pete's state of mind. "I have to focus on Rob right now. Pete's a grown man, Betsy. He'll have to figure this out on his own." She was hurt and angry and very tired of giving Pete Fleming the benefit of the doubt.

She pulled into the emergency-room parking lot and ran the short distance to the reception desk. "Robert Turner," she said breathlessly. "Gunshot wound to the shoulder?"

The desk clerk glanced up at her and held up one finger. He was on the phone.

"Just put them in the microwave then." He gave Amanda a smile and started turning pages on a clipboard, then stopped. "No. You have to take it out of that pan and—"

"Oh, for pity's sake," Amanda said and took the clipboard away from him.

"Hey, there are rules. You can't do that, lady. Don't you know about HIPAA?" He jerked the clipboard away from her. "Are you family?"

"I'm his guardian," she replied and hoped God would forgive the slight stretch of truth.

The desk clerk ran his finger down the entries on the clipboard. "He's on his way to surgery." He nodded toward the far end of the hall where an aide was pushing a gurney toward the elevators and a familiar figure was keeping pace alongside.

Pete.

"Thanks," Amanda called as she ran down the long hall dodging carts and hospital workers as she went. She caught up with them just as the elevator doors opened.

Rob was a little groggy but he recognized her. "Hi, Amanda," he said in a slurred voice. "They're gonna take out the bullet and Pete says I'm going to get a commendation from the mayor and Mama's gonna be so proud and—"

"Shhh. We'll talk later." She grasped his hand and held on. The orderly looked confused. "Well, let's go," Amanda said.

The orderly stepped inside and pushed the button. Amanda focused all her attention on Rob, ignoring Pete. Her emotions were in such a jumble that she couldn't decide if she wanted to hug Pete or yell at him.

The elevator bell dinged as the doors opened, shaking her back to the moment at hand.

"I'm afraid this is the end of the line for you folks," the orderly said. "You can wait in there. The doctor will come out when it's over."

Amanda leaned down and kissed Rob's cheek.

"Say a prayer for me," he whispered.

She fought back tears as she nodded.

Rob turned his attention to Pete. "If anything happens, you take Amanda with you to tell Mama, okay?"

"Nothing's going to happen except you're going to come out of there with a bullet for a souvenir," Pete assured him and grasped Rob's hand tightly.

"Maybe so, but it'd be good if you could pray with Amanda here. Mama says that God gets pretty busy around these holiday times—extra prayers can't hurt."

Pete made a sound that was sort of a laugh and Amanda glanced at him for the first time. His eyes were filled with tears but he was smiling at Rob. "I'm not sure God would recognize my voice, champ."

"That's not a bad thing. Surprise Him to hear from you after all this time. He's more likely to listen up."

"Folks," the orderly interrupted.

Amanda kissed Rob once more and let him go. The automatic doors opened and beyond them she saw the activity of hospital staff preparing for the surgery. The sight of Rob alone in the midst of all that equipment and cold sterile light was her breaking point. She released the tears of exhaustion and fear that she'd held in check throughout the last long hours.

Chapter Thirteen

Without a word, Pete wrapped his arms around her and led her into the empty waiting room. He helped her to a worn sofa, then switched off the blare of a reality show replay on the television and got them both coffee from the machine in the corner. When he handed her the cup, her hand shook so badly that the hot liquid sloshed over the top of the cup and onto her fingers. She gave no sign she had even noticed.

"Here," Pete said and set the cup aside while he wiped her hand with tissues from the box on the side table. He dumped half the coffee into a nearby plant and handed it to her again. "Try some. It's not that bad."

She gripped the cup with both hands and brought it to her lips. Then she sat with her head down, her shoulders releasing the occasional aftershock of her crying, and said nothing.

"He's going to be fine," Pete said. He was at a total loss for words. There was so much he wanted to say, so much he needed her to know, to understand.

"Why did you come?" she asked, still not looking at him.

"I needed to see for myself that he's okay."

"And then?"

"Then I don't know. All I know is that I need to get my life back on track, and I think I need to start by going back to Chicago. It's time I stop licking my wounds and take responsibility for things that have happened."

"You're determined to take the blame for Rob's injury." Her voice was flat and tired as if she had no fight left.

Pete sat next to her on the sofa. "I *am* responsible, Amanda. He wouldn't have been there if I hadn't come up with this idea for getting the real thief."

"Did you know it was Jake?"

"I knew there was someone older pulling the strings. There was something about the way Jake was always with Travis."

"And Chad."

"No. He got mixed up in it later. I told you that once the others knew his background, he would be a target and that he wouldn't be strong enough to stand up for himself. That's one of the reasons I spent so much time with him."

"Then that piece of it is my fault."

"No. Chad came by the boathouse one day when I wasn't expecting him. I was cleaning the gun and didn't see him there on the deck watching me."

"So it was Chad who took your gun?"

"I'm sure he didn't take it, but he did tell Jake that it was there."

"But he didn't see you hide it. He couldn't have seen that from the deck."

Pete shrugged. "He saw enough. I went up to the loft with the gun and came back without it. The boathouse doesn't have too many hiding places. Jake would have had no trouble figuring it out. He's a smart kid."

"So you're determined to take this all on yourself."

He took her by the shoulders, surprising her so that she finally looked directly at him. "Amanda, I've been thinking about maybe getting out of police work. Call it burnout or anything you like, but I'm finished."

"Well, that's a step."

"The problem is I've never done anything else and if I can ever hope to have any peace in my life, I have to—"

"Then let me help you." Her words were a plea, her voice cracking with emotion.

He held up his fingers in the sign for "I love you." "Did you mean that?" he asked.

Tears spilled down her cheeks and all she could do was nod. Pete let out a breath that felt as if he'd been holding it for the last hour. To her it must have sounded like a breath of exasperation.

"It's okay," she said pulling free of his hands and walking to the window. "I mean, love isn't always a two-way street and that's okay. Just know that love can—"

"I love you, Amanda. From the minute I heard your name it was like one of those songs you get in your head and can't figure out why it stays there. I think I fell in love with you before I even knew you, when I was watching you try and put the pier in by yourself. At that moment I knew you were different from any woman I'd known."

"We could do this together, Pete. Start by telling me about that night. Tell me all of it."

The last thing Pete wanted to do—especially on this night—was to go back to that other shooting. On the other hand, she deserved to know. After all, she'd trusted him with her story. He cleared his throat and realized he was nervous.

"I'm not sure where to begin."

"What was the case?"

"It wasn't an actual case we were working on, just a good tip that something was going down—like tonight."

She nodded. "Any other similarities to tonight?"

"There was a festival—a street festival in one of the inner-city neighborhoods—Juneteenth Day."

"So lots of people and noise and hoopla?"

"Yeah. And firecrackers." It was a lot like earlier tonight, he thought. "Jud and I were working the crowd undercover. We'd had a tip about these two gangs—one was planning to attack the other at the festival. Random stuff—a knifing in the crowd perhaps or someone shot. We couldn't be sure what we were looking for."

"Did you know *who* you were looking for?"

"Yeah. But the kids are wise to that. They wear hooded sweatshirts that cover their faces. It's hard to know who's who."

In his memory, he saw the scene, heard the noise of excited conversation, heard the pop of the firecrackers, the music, the shouts above the rest of the noise. He smelled the food cooking on smoky grills up and down the street. He closed his eyes.

"Then," he continued, "I saw him—the kid we needed to get to before anything happened. He saw me about the same time and started to move through the crowd, trying to get away."

"Where was Jud?"

"Parallel to me. The kid was between us. We were closing in. Then out of nowhere I saw this other kid coming, saw the flash of metal in his hand, saw the perp take cover by putting this new kid between himself and me."

"What did you do?" Her voice was gentle.

"I—ah—I pulled out my weapon and shouted for the kid to drop his, all the time moving toward him fast as Jud did the same from the other side." Pete felt his breath coming in short gasps, like that night when the adrenaline had coursed through his veins. "Again I shouted, 'Police! Drop your weapon!'"

"And what did the boy do?"

"The one I thought was carrying the gun just looked at me with this surprised look. Then I saw a flash, felt the bullet in my thigh, went down and fired."

They were quiet for a long moment. Amanda stroked Pete's back and his breathing gradually came back to normal.

"It was the other kid—the one you were chasing in the first place—who fired the gun, right?"

Pete nodded. "He was using the kid for cover."

"What was in the kid's hand? I mean, you saw him carrying something."

"A soda can." He drew in a shuddering breath as he saw again the boy lying there on the street. "It got so quiet," he whispered, remembering. "Like everything had just frozen for that minute. Then there was this scream and his mother pushed through the crowd and saw her son."

"And she held him the way I was holding Rob earlier, and she looked up at you," Amanda guessed.

"Yeah. The look in her eyes." His voice was raspy and barely audible.

"But it wasn't your fault," Amanda said. "There was a gun. You were in danger."

"There was an investigation, of course," Pete went on as if she hadn't spoken. "They called it self-defense. Even the neighborhood leaders agreed that the kid was a decoy for the real shooter. And it was—he was—but—"

"Pete, it was the boy you were chasing who put that other boy in danger. He hid behind that innocent child. He shot you even after you showed your weapon and ordered him twice to surrender."

Pete looked at her for the first time since beginning his recounting of the shooting. "You didn't see the way she looked at me," he said. "That mother—"

"Pete, she would have looked at God Himself that way. In that instant that she lost her son, she saw not only what he had been to her, but all that she had dreamed for him. The better life. The opportunities. The years they were going to have together. In a single gunshot, all of that was gone."

"Is that what you felt?"

"Of course I did. I was furious for weeks and months. I stuffed it all inside, not being able to even cry for them, I was so angry at the unfairness of it all."

"But in time you got past it. I mean, you're sad and you miss them, but you seem—okay."

She smiled. "I have my good days and bad. Luckily the good now far outweighs the bad."

"I'm looking forward to that."

She wrapped her arms around him and put her head

on his shoulder. "I have some words of wisdom I can share if you like."

"I don't think I'm up to scripture quotes," he said gently.

She laughed. "Oh, Pete, you have so much to learn about how God communicates with us in this world."

"Detective? Ms. Hunter?" The doctor stood just inside the door, still in his operating scrubs. "The surgery went fine. No damage that won't heal. He's in recovery."

"May we see him?" Amanda had rushed to the door the minute she saw the doctor.

"As soon as they get him to his room. He'll be pretty groggy tonight, but in the morning I expect he'll be sore but wide awake."

"Thank you," Amanda said. "He's such a good kid, doctor."

"Well, he's a strong kid, I'll give him that. He had to have been in a lot of pain and he lost a lot of blood, but the worst is behind him. I'll stop by to see him tomorrow."

After the doctor left, Amanda turned back to Pete. "Will you stay?"

"For now." He put his arm around her shoulders. "Let's go find his room and wait for him."

Rob was awake when they brought him in and transferred him to a normal hospital bed. By that time Amanda had called the camp and assured herself that everything was fine. "I'm going to stay with him tonight," Pete heard her tell Dottie Roark. "There's a recliner. I can sleep there." She paused to listen. "He's here. See you tomorrow."

She hung up the phone and hovered around the foot of the bed while the transfer was made. Rob grinned at her and held up a small piece of metal. "Souvenir," he slurred with a big grin.

While Amanda fussed over the covers and pillows, Pete cornered the nurse. "Here's my cell-phone number. Are you on the rest of the night?"

She nodded. "Call me if anything changes and you can't find me—this kid spikes a fever, I want to know, okay?"

"We really can't give that information to anyone but family," she began.

"I'm his arresting officer," Pete interrupted. "He's critical to a big case in Chicago."

The nurse's expression told him he had succeeded in impressing her. She took the number and stuck it in her pocket. Pete turned his attention to Rob.

"Hey, Pete," Rob said, drawing out the name as if it had multiple syllables.

Pete sat on the side of the bed and gave the kid a high five. "Good work tonight, Rob."

"Think I might make a good detective?"

"I think you need some sleep and the two of you can discuss this tomorrow," Amanda interrupted.

"Better listen to the boss," Pete said with a grin.

Something about that seemed hysterically funny to Rob. He started to giggle and pretty soon Amanda and Pete were laughing with him.

"There's a call for you at the desk, Detective," the nurse said. "Shall I have it transferred in here?"

"No, I'll come out there." He gave Amanda's hand a squeeze and went to take the call. It was the captain, checking in to be sure everything was under control and to see how Rob had come through surgery.

"Jud was impressed with the kid," he told Pete, "and frankly, so was I. After the two of you left the office the other night, I did a background check."

"He's not a bad kid, Captain."

"No. He's like a lot of them—smart, but no place to be except the street. I looked up the case notes you did on him. Seemed to me like he gave you a real run for your money when it came to mouthing off."

Pete smiled at the memory of the tall skinny kid Rob had been in those days. Scared to death but covering it up with a truckload of attitude and street smarts. Like Travis, he thought.

"Well, thanks to Amanda, he made it out alive. I think he'll be okay."

"Yeah. I guess one is better than none. What about the others—those two who pulled the robbery and the kid who was the lookout?"

"Jake Buntrock was pulling the strings, Captain."

"Yet every one of them has a record of his own," Bingle reminded him.

"Even so, at that age there might be a way to turn them around. The kid who was the lookout helped when he could have—"

"Look, Fleming, nobody wishes we could save more of these kids than I do. If you can come up with a plan, I'm willing to listen. The mayor's been on my back for months about what he calls 'traditional police methods' not working."

"The mayor ought to talk to Amanda. I'll bet she could give him a couple of ideas."

"Until then," the captain continued, "we play everything strictly by the book, understood?"

"Understood," Pete replied. "One favor, though."

"Name it."

"Rob's mom—"

"Aunt Betsy already called me on that one. I've arranged for one of the officers to pick her up and drive her there to the hospital. Anything else?"

"If old man Devereaux is willing not to press charges, can the younger boys stay and finish the camp session? There's only a week left and it might do them some good."

There was silence for so long on the other end that Pete thought that maybe the captain had hung up.

"There's the gun, Fleming," he said finally. "You've got a kid lying there in the hospital."

"Separate charge. It was Jake who took my gun, kidnapped Amanda—all that can be separated from the robbery."

"I'll talk to Devereaux, but—"

"Let Betsy talk to him first, okay?"

"They can't stand each other," Bingle protested.

Pete smiled. "Maybe—maybe not. Give her a shot at it."

"All right. But I'm going to need a full report on my desk first thing Monday, understood?"

"Got it. Thanks," Pete added and hung up.

He had planned to leave once he knew Rob was all right. But now he wanted to—needed to—stay. He needed to think through the evening's events. More than that, he needed to consider where he would go from here, and how his life could include Amanda.

It was nearly midnight and the halls were deserted, but the waiting room was across from the nurses' station. He could hear the staff talking and laughing as they went about their work. Pete needed a place where he wouldn't be interrupted. He passed Rob's room and paused.

Amanda was curled up in the recliner fast asleep. He used an extra blanket to cover her and then turned to check on Rob. What struck him was the way Rob's features had relaxed in sleep. For the first time all summer, he looked like the sixteen-year-old kid that he was, his face finally free of the constant tension and suspicion that had made him look years older. Pete reached down and pulled the covers higher around the boy. Amanda was right. These were children—his children, hers, the captain's—children of the street for the most part, whose only crime had been their birthright. Surely there was some way—

He walked to the end of the hall toward an open door. The brass plate on the wall read Children's Wing Chapel. The room was small with a few rows of uphol-stered chairs facing an altar decorated with fresh flow-ers. Behind the altar were stained-glass windows, lit from behind. One featured a dove of peace. The other a pair of heavenly hands reaching forward toward a crowd of children of all races and ages. The text was, *Suffer the little children to come unto me.*

Pete stared at the inscription on a small brass plate just beneath the window that featured the children: Given in loving memory of Daniel Hunter by the Elizabeth Bin-gle Foundation. He looked at the plate under the window featuring the peace dove. That was in honor of Stanley Hunter—Amanda's husband and Danny's father. Had Amanda helped in the selection of those tributes?

Pete sat down heavily in the front row of chairs and stared at the hands beckoning the children. He sat there for a long time. For much of that time his breathing sounded like the exhausted heaves of a man on the last leg of an Iron Man race. He couldn't seem to stop replaying everything that had happened and had almost happened. Again and again the image of that gun muzzle pressed to Amanda's temple flashed through his mind. Each time it did, he felt his heart slam against his chest and then stop as it had at the scene. The more he replayed those moments, the more they faded in and out with that other night when he had stared down at a dead kid and back up into the accusing eyes of the boy's mother.

He remembered Amanda saying earlier, "You didn't know him—he was a stranger. And yet you felt the pain of his loss. When you looked into the eyes of the boy's mother, what you saw reflected there was the loss of the future she had planned for her son."

Remembering the future. What if, instead of sitting here relieved that everything had turned out all right, he were sitting here trying to accept that Amanda was dead?

All those thoughts he'd entertained about "some day" with Amanda—some day after I get things figured out. Some day when the time is right for both of us. Some day when she's had time to get over the loss of her husband and son. Some day when I have more to offer.

Tonight they had come dangerously close to losing all those somedays. And Pete knew, with a certainty he had never thought possible, that God had led him to this moment. With God's love he could find forgiveness, and with God's strength he could be the man that Amanda deserved.

Pete had to figure out a way that they could share a life now if Amanda was willing, and he had to do it on her turf. There was no question of asking her to give up the camp and come live his so-called life. She was the one who had it together. His job was to figure out a way to fit into that.

He stared at the stained-glass piece and the inscription below for several long moments. Then he took out his ever-present notepad and wrote down two words: *Danny's Place.*

When Amanda woke, it was still dark and the wall clock showed quarter to four. She pushed aside the blanket, then realized that Pete must have covered her and pulled it close again, as if wrapping herself in it would bring him closer. Rob was sleeping peacefully. *"Thank you,"* she whispered. *"Thank you, God, for keeping him safe, for keeping us all safe. I know I've asked for a lot lately, but please be with Jake and the others, especially Jake. He has lost his way so badly and I don't know how to help him."*

Amanda stared at Rob for a long time, imagining the horrific possibilities of what might have happened earlier. How could she have misjudged Jake so badly? How could she not have seen that the camp clown was in such pain?

Because you had your own pain to deal with.

That's no excuse.

No, that's life. Sometimes like the weather, clouds roll in and block our ability to see very far in front of us.

Still—

It's done. Learn from it and move forward.

She thought about how in just a few short days this

year's campers would head back to the city, back to the lives and the pressures they had known before they came to her. Always her prayer on that last day was that somehow she and her staff had managed to give them tools they could use to defuse some of that pressure. Tools that would make them stop and think and have the courage to stand up and go against the gang or the bully or the system that expected so little of them.

She had long wished that somehow there might be a way to expand the program to something year-round. Oh, she wasn't about to abandon the camp, but if there could be a counterpart to that in the city—a place where these boys knew they could go and get exactly what they had gotten this summer.

She had it all planned out—had done that piece of it with Stan. All she needed was a place and the funding and the support of the court system and a staff and the time and—

She slumped back down onto the edge of the chair and clutched the blanket. It was all so hard and it was all so very lonely. She had friends, of course—but they had lives of their own, children of their own, plans of their own. Since Stan and Danny had drowned she had made the camp her life. Then Pete Fleming had come along and made her long for those other pieces that make a life whole—companionship, a partner to plan and build things with, love.

Please God, if he's going to stop being a detective, let him want to do this work with me. Let him stay and be in my life.

She heard voices in the hall, so hastily ended her prayer and stood to fold the blanket.

Rob's mother did not even see Amanda at first. Her eyes were on her son. She hurried to his bedside and touched his forehead with a heartbreaking tenderness.

"Robbie," she whispered and her voice shook. In spite of the fact that it was still hot and humid outside, she wore a light coat that looked several sizes too large for her, except for the too-short sleeves. She was a tall angular woman, graceful as a dancer. Amanda could not help but think that she must have been a true beauty before the ravages of her cancer and the life she faced had taken their toll.

Satisfied that her son was only sleeping, she looked up and when she saw Amanda, held out her arms.

"Amanda," she said as the two women embraced. "I should have known you wouldn't leave him."

"He's going to be fine, Ella."

"The officer told me all about it. He said my Rob is a hero." She looked back at Rob and smiled. "I bet you wouldn't have thought that a couple of years ago when he first came here."

Amanda smiled. "He was always smart, Ella. He just needed a little 'redirection.'"

Both women chuckled at that. Rob needing redirection had been Ella's plea to the judge and to Amanda when she'd ask for Rob to be sent to camp instead of jail.

Amanda pulled the chair she'd been using closer to the bed. "Here, Ella. Why don't you sit with him and get some rest yourself? I could use a cup of coffee. Can I get you anything?"

Ella shook her head as she removed her coat and folded it over the back of the chair. "No, thanks. You go on home now."

"You know me better than that, Ella." She saw that Ella was exhausted. "You're the one who needs your rest." She guided Ella into the chair and showed her how to make it recline. "We can't have Rob waking up and worrying about you." She patted Ella's hand and placed the light blanket over her, then tiptoed toward the door.

"Amanda? Thank that detective for me, okay? Rob wrote me about him. He must be a very special man. He's been so good to my boy. So good—"

Ella was asleep and so was Rob. Amanda went to find Pete.

"Have you seen Detective Fleming?" she asked the nurse.

"I think I saw him go into the chapel at the end of the hall earlier, but that was around midnight and I haven't seen him since."

"Thanks." Amanda followed the direction the nurse had indicated and quietly opened the door to the chapel. Pete sat in the first row, his back to her, his shoulders hunched. As she moved closer, she saw that he was writing. She paused. Every once in a while he would look up at the stained-glass window in front of him and then start writing again. From the looks of it, he had already filled several pages of the small notebook.

"Pete? I thought—" I was so afraid that you had gone.

He turned and in the soft light of the room, his face bathed in tears, his smile was radiant with what she could only describe as pure joy. "Amanda, I've found the answer right here."

Her heart sang as she hurried to take the seat next to his and touch his wet cheeks. "Oh, Pete, I'm so happy for you."

He looked confused and then laughed. "For the kids," he said. "I've got an idea for saving the kids—Antwone, Chad, Travis and dozens more."

"But they're safe, Pete." She reached for him.

He stepped away, shaking his head in denial. "Not just tonight, Amanda. For the future. Tell me what more would you do for these kids if you could?"

"Oh, Pete. There's so much. You know that, but everything costs money and—"

"Listen to this, okay?"

The words spilled out of his mouth as the tears must have spilled down his cheeks. Like the camp but all year long. Part in the city and then summers at the camp. Funding from Betsy and Winnie and even Devereaux. The captain and the mayor demanding alternative ideas. Programs involving not only the boys, but the community, the churches, the businesses, the families.

Amanda let him talk. He made it all sound so real—so possible. Of course, she should have expected that he would deny any spiritual breakthrough for himself. But Amanda saw God's hand in this, heard God's breath in the rush of words and ideas, saw God's radiance in Pete's eyes.

"And we'll call it Danny's Place," he said finally and waited for her response. When it didn't come right away, he added, "Is that okay?"

Amanda didn't hesitate. She placed her hands on his cheeks and kissed him. "I love you so very much, Pete Fleming."

He looked at her with that crooked half smile she had come to treasure. "Down the road, Amanda, I'm going to want to ask you to marry me. I know it's too soon, but—"

"If you ask me now, I'll say yes," she said softly. She saw him glance at the memorials to Stan and Danny. "And they would both give their blessings," she added.

"You're sure?" It was the first time she had ever seen him so openly uncertain.

"About what?" she replied. "You have to actually ask the question, you know."

"I'm not a get-down-on-one-knee romantic," he warned.

"No kidding?" she said in mock surprise.

"I can be hard to live with— I've been on my own a long time and I'm pretty set in my ways."

"We'll have to work on that. Luckily I have experience working with young men who think they have all the answers."

He frowned and ducked his head and when he raised it again, he was smiling. "Then I guess I've run out of warnings. Amanda Hunter, will you marry me?"

"I will."

They stood there grinning at each other like two teenagers who had just discovered first love as the room grew lighter with the dawn of a new day. And then Pete kissed her and this time she had no doubt that it was a kiss filled with love and promises for their future together.

Epilogue

Four years later

Jake Buntrock sat in the warden's office. The warden was completing the paperwork. Jake was used to waiting. He'd gotten very good at it in the four years he'd served in the medium-security Sturtevant Prison.

Around him he could hear the now-familiar sounds of prison life—the men in the exercise yard, the opening and closing of gates and the jangle of the alarm signifying time to get back to work. In the early days, he'd hated those sounds, each one jarring in a different way. Then gradually and with help, he'd settled in to pay for his crime.

Amanda had come every week. For the first three months, he refused to see her or speak with her, so she sent letters. Eventually he decided she was going to haunt him forever, so he might as well see her. And so began a weekly ritual supported in between by letters and phone calls that saw him through the four years. Four years that changed his life.

One time when she couldn't come because she was pregnant and her doctor wanted her to take it easy, she'd sent Pete Fleming. The last person Jake had ever thought he would confide in was the detective. And yet, he would never forget that day as long as he lived.

On that cold, rainy March day Jake had been bored and the four-year sentence stretched before him like an endless nightmare. Pete Fleming pulled some strings and saw him in the warden's office. The warden left them alone.

Pete sat in an armchair, one ankle crossed over the opposite knee. Jake stood at the window watching the rain.

"You didn't have to come," Jake muttered.

"You're right. I didn't. So why do you think I did?"

"Amanda made you."

Pete laughed. "We don't play that game. Guess again."

Jake shrugged.

"I came because I needed to see you. I needed to try and figure out what kind of hurt you were in to do what you did. I wanted to see if maybe I could forgive you and help you get on with your life."

Jake turned around. "Why would you do that?"

"Let's just say I spent a lot of my twenties being ticked off at the rest of the world—a little like you are. I'd like to help you avoid wasting those years."

Then it was Jake's turn to laugh. "I'm in prison, man."

Pete shrugged. "A lot of people walking around outside these walls are in prisons of their own making. You were in prison way before you got sent here."

Jake had fought against the tears he'd held back for weeks. Pete slid a chair across the floor and motioned for him to sit. "Come on. Let's talk this through."

Over the course of three hours that afternoon and in weekly visits separate from Amanda's, Pete and Jake talked. They talked about fathers who don't seem to know how to love their sons. They talked about fears. They talked about that night at the Devereaux place. And they talked about Jake's future. After a month, Jake had started classes to continue his interrupted college education. After a year, he'd decided to change his major to social work. After two years he was working with prison counselors, developing alternative programs for other prisoners.

Amanda's visits always ended in prayer and a hug. His visits with Pete ended with a handshake and a challenge to go further. The combination saved his life.

"You ready, son?" the warden asked as he came around his desk and opened the door of his office.

Jake stood. "Yes, sir."

The warden smiled and extended his hand. "It's always strange when I find myself telling a prisoner that he'll be missed, but if you ever think about using that social work degree of yours to do prison counseling, give me a call first, okay?"

Jake smiled. "That's not real likely, sir, but I'll keep it in mind."

The warden laughed and pounded him on the back as he led him out to the outer office. Pete was sitting on the edge of the desk, talking to the warden's assistant.

"Well, here it is, Jake," he said. "Independence Day."

Jake could not keep the grin off his face as he walked through the yard and out the gates for the last time.

"Are you going to be okay with going back to camp?"

"You mean revisit the scene of the crime, Detective?" Jake threw his stuff into the back seat and started to get in on the passenger side. "Might as well find out."

"I'm not a detective and I'm definitely not your chauffeur, kid." Pete tossed him the keys. "You drive."

Jake put the car in gear and eased away from the curb. He kept his gaze firmly focused on the road ahead. He had no mixed emotions about leaving the medium-security prison where he'd spent the last four years.

"Do you miss it? Being a detective and all?" he asked Pete.

"Nope. It's no life for a family man."

Jake nodded. "I'm going to have to look for work now."

"Well, unless you have an interview that I don't know about today, you can lose the tie," Pete said, grinning at him.

Jake fumbled with the knot and removed the tie. Then he steered with his knees and rolled back the sleeves of his cotton dress shirt.

"Hands on the wheel, champ," Pete said, but he was smiling.

When they reached the outskirts of Racine, Pete cut off the air-conditioning and rolled down the windows. He didn't say why. He didn't have to. Jake knew that he was offering him the smell of fresh air—the smell of freedom.

"Amanda didn't come," Jake said finally. It was a statement rather than a question.

"She'll see you at camp. You know how it is. The kids keep her hopping."

Jake nodded. "I was sorry to hear about Miss Bingle."

"She didn't suffer a bit," Pete assured him. "Just went to sleep one afternoon looking out at the lake and didn't wake up."

"She was a really special lady. Is her friend still there?"

"Winnie? For the summer, but in September, she's getting married. Want to take a guess who the lucky groom is?"

"How would I know?"

"Oh, you know him. Come on—take a guess."

Even after four years of Pete never missing a week visiting him, it still seemed strange to have the man treat him like a friend—an equal.

"Well?" Pete prompted.

"I give up."

"Walter Devereaux."

"Yeah, right." Jake glanced at Pete and saw that the man was serious. "Really? How—I mean—he's really old and—"

"Well, Winnie's no blushing bride."

Jake shook his head. Then he grinned. Then he started to laugh out loud, and so did Pete and it felt wonderful.

"It's partly your fault," Pete told him. "The old man came storming over to Betsy's the day after the break-in, demanding that something be done about shutting down the camp."

"And?"

"And Betsy wasn't there, but Winnie was. Apparently, she charmed the socks off the old guy—sympathized with the trauma he'd been through, got him lemonade and some of her terrific brownies and sat him down to wait for Betsy. While they sat there, she started talking to him, asking him all sorts of questions about himself as a boy and then taking note of the similarities with Chad at that same age."

"What happened when Miss Bingle got there?"

"Nothing. The old man had gone home to change so he and Winnie could go to dinner. After that night, they were inseparable. She even got him to volunteer at the camp."

Jake couldn't imagine the proper old dude at camp. "Doing what?"

"Turns out he's quite a musician, so he helps out there."

Jake just shook his head. He leaned his face out the open window, enjoying the rush of air. He'd dreamed of this day for four years, but strangely enough, he didn't regret those years. He regretted getting himself sent to prison in the first place for sure, and it had taken most of the first year for him to accept that he was going to do the time.

"You know Miss Bingle came to see me."

It was Pete's turn to be surprised. "I don't think even Amanda knew that."

"She came about every six months or so. Seemed like just when I'd about given up on her coming back, there she was."

"You never mentioned it—I mean, when Amanda or I came."

"Miss Bingle asked me not to." He smiled. "She was something. A real class act. All the guys who saw her said that—it was like without even meeting her, they understood."

"What did you two talk about?"

Jake shrugged. "Books. She'd bring me these books and tell me to read them and we'd discuss them on her next visit. Only her idea of discussion was to grill me about the characters and the plot and the messages. And then she'd say something like, 'And what did you learn from this, Jacob?'—she never called me Jake. I'd tell her. She'd smile and leave."

"And what did you learn?"

"She said that I was learning how to take the next step. She always talked about how prison could either be a lifestyle for me or an enriching experience. Believe me, I thought she was downright crazy the first time she threw that one at me. In fact, I laughed in her face. But she just kept coming back." His voice trailed off as he remembered the visits. "The funny thing was she always seemed to know just what was bothering me."

Pete nodded as they turned onto the road leading to the camp. "Yeah. She did that for me, too."

Every time a car passed, Amanda ran to the window.

"Mommy, you're gonna wear that carpet," Ty warned.

She looked down at her three-year-old son, tiny lines furrowing his forehead. He was a miniature version of his father.

"It's wear a *hole* in the carpet," his twin sister, Lizzie, said with an exasperated sigh. The kid was three going on thirty.

"Hey, you two, come here and let me look at you."

"Ah, Mom," Ty protested, but he came.

"Now then, Jake might be a little shy. It's been a while since he—"

"We know," Lizzie said, "it's been a long time since Jake had a party." She smiled. "We know how to make it fun, Mommy. He can play with us."

Boo woke from his afternoon nap and raced to the door. Amanda hadn't heard a thing and here they were. She took one last look around and went to meet them.

She held out her arms to Jake and he grinned and ran up the steps to greet her.

"You're too thin," she said, laughing as he swung her around.

"Maybe, but I'm free and ready to start the rest of my life thanks to you."

She stopped laughing and cupped his face with her hands. "We didn't do anything, Jake. You did it. You turned your life around." Tears welled in her eyes. When she thought about how far this boy—this young man—had come in four short years….

"Are we gonna have a party or not?" Ty asked.

Pete scooped him high in his arms and tickled him until he dissolved into giggles. "Party time!" he shouted and both kids took up the cry.

Lizzie tugged on Jake's leg and motioned for him to come closer. He knelt down so she could whisper in his ear. Amanda caught the words "Lots of surprises."

"Really?" Jake said and looked shocked. "Must be for some other guy."

"No, all for you," Lizzie assured him.

Amanda watched Jake with her children. He was laughing and teasing them. Like the old Jake, the real Jake—not the camp clown who had covered up pain and anger.

"Come, let's go," she said, taking his arm while Pete, the children and Boo brought up the rear.

"Hey, where is everybody?" Jake asked as they walked down the hill to the mess hall. "It's pretty quiet around here for the middle of summer."

"They're all in there," Ty shouted excitedly.

Lizzie rolled her eyes.

They walked into the mess hall and everyone stood and applauded as Amanda led Jake to the front of the room. She handed him a graduation cap and gown.

"What is all this?" he asked, but he was laughing and he immediately put on the gown.

"Your graduation," Dottie Roark said as she placed the cap on his head. Then she signaled the music counselor to strike up "Pomp and Circumstance."

The ceremony was brief and beautiful. Amanda and Dottie both cried when Rob handed Jake the degree in Social Work that he had earned while serving his sentence. Jake cried when he took the microphone and tried to speak. He made several false starts and then handed the microphone back to Rob and took his seat.

"I think what Jake wants to tell you guys," Rob said, "is that he sat where you're sitting. He got a chance and he messed that up, big-time. And then, because she believes in guys like us, Amanda gave him another chance. And this time, he took it and ran with it. You guys should be so lucky."

"Party!" Ty shouted and the campers took up the cry.

"Hold your horses," Edna yelled as she came through the swinging doors from the kitchen. She was carrying a pan filled with fresh steaming corn on the cob. "Well, don't just sit there. Help me get this food out."

"How do you think he's doing? Is this too much?" Amanda asked Pete as they stood together later watching Jake with Rob and the other counselors.

"Well, honey, if he's having trouble with this, he's going to flip out when you spring the rest on him."

"Maybe it's too much."

Pete tucked her hair behind her ear. "You're not having second thoughts, are you?"

"No. Well, maybe."

"Look at him. He's a natural."

She smiled and touched his cheek. "Is this the same man who just four years ago thought they ought to throw away the key?"

"I know. Somewhere in there somebody taught me about trust and forgiveness." He pressed her palm to his lips and gave her the sign for "I love you." "Go on. Ask him." He gave her a gentle push toward Jake.

"Hi, Jake, having fun?" Amanda handed him a serving of strawberry shortcake and sat across from him.

"They look so young," he said, and laughed.

Amanda shrugged. "Well, you remember how it was. You were young but you felt old. You felt like you needed to take on the world because there was no one else to fight for you."

Jake sobered and picked at his cake. "Yeah."

"Have you heard from your father?"

He shook his head. "He sent his lawyer to the prison about a month ago. There were some papers, something about a fund but the deal was that I'm to disappear—at least from his life."

Amanda covered his hand with hers. "I'm sorry, Jake."

He shrugged and resumed eating his cake.

"I'd— That is, Pete and I would like it if you would consider coming back to work for us."

"You mean here?"

"Well, here and in the city in the year-round program. I mean, you went to all the trouble to get that degree and all."

"Why would you do that? Why would the detective do that?"

"Ex-detective, son," Pete reminded him as he joined them. "I work for this beautiful lady these days."

"*With* me, not for me," she corrected.

Pete straddled the picnic bench next to Jake. "Look, here's the deal. We need a social worker to help us in counseling and getting kids into the program. You have this brand-new social-work degree plus you have all this experience—admittedly, we could have done without some of it, but God works in mysterious ways as Miss Bingle used to say."

Jake looked from one to the other and back again. He was speechless.

"Well?" Amanda asked and she was smiling.

"You'd do that for me?"

"We'd do it for the kids, Jake," she replied softly. "You can help them."

"I'd sure like to try."

"Looks like we got us a social worker, Mrs. Fleming."

"Come meet the rest of the staff," Amanda said.

The party continued all afternoon. As the sun was setting, Amanda watched while Jake helped the counselors build the campfire. Pete came up behind her and wrapped his arms around her. "Happy?"

"You know, I was just thinking about that. Do you remember that night at the hospital?"

"Let me see—there was this chapel and—"

"Yeah, well, I thought that was the happiest night of my life. And then there was your acceptance of God into your life, and our wedding day. And then the twins and the realization of Danny's Place and—" She turned around and hugged him tight. "It just keeps getting better and better," she whispered.

"Well, you were the one who brought up all that 'remembering the future' business. I figured if I kept one step ahead of the future by making every day count, then we'd have no regrets."

"It's working because right now—this minute—I have never been happier."

Pete glanced up to Heaven and made the sign for "Thank you," and then he kissed her.

* * * * *

Dear Reader,

This book is the last project I worked on with my friend, mentor and longtime agent, Jane Jordan Browne. Jane died in February 2003, after a short illness. In all of the conversations we had about the novel, Jane never mentioned that one of her passions was her support of a similar camp for troubled youths. I found that out only after I had completed the novel. That was so typical of her unassuming and generous spirit. She taught me so much—not just about writing—but about life. Without realizing it, I modeled Amanda's influence on her young campers on Jane's influence on me and countless others. I hope you have someone in your life like that—someone who, like Amanda in this novel and Jane in real life, can see beyond the shell and facade.

All best,

Anna Schmidt

Send someone a little Inspiration this Easter with…

Take 2 inspirational love stories FREE!

PLUS get a FREE surprise gift!

Mail to Steeple Hill Reader Service™

In U.S.
3010 Walden Ave.
P.O. Box 1867
Buffalo, NY 14240-1867

In Canada
P.O. Box 609
Fort Erie, Ontario
L2A 5X3

YES! Please send me 2 free Love Inspired® novels and my free surprise gift. After receiving them, if I don't wish to receive anymore, I can return the shipping statement marked cancel. If I don't cancel, I will receive 4 brand-new novels every month, before they're available in stores! Bill me at the low price of $4.24 each in the U.S. and $4.74 each in Canada, plus 25¢ shipping and handling and applicable sales tax, if any*. That's the complete price and a savings of over 10% off the cover prices—quite a bargain! I understand that accepting the books and gift places me under no obligation ever to buy any books. I can always return a shipment and cancel at any time. Even if I never buy another book from Steeple Hill, the 2 free books and the surprise gift are mine to keep forever.

113 IDN DZ9M
313 IDN DZ9N

Name	(PLEASE PRINT)	
Address	Apt. No.	
City	State/Prov.	Zip/Postal Code

Not valid to current Love Inspired® subscribers.

Want to try two free books from another series?
Call 1-800-873-8635 or visit www.morefreebooks.com.

* Terms and prices are subject to change without notice. Sales tax applicable in New York. Canadian residents will be charged applicable provincial taxes and GST. All orders subject to approval. Offer limited to one per household.

® are registered trademarks owned and used by the trademark owner and or its licensee.

INTLI04R   ©2004 Steeple Hill

Love Inspired

THE McKASLIN CLAN

SERIES CONTINUES WITH...

SWEET BLESSINGS

BY

JILLIAN HART

Single mom Amy McKaslin welcomed newcomer Heath Murdock into her family diner after he'd shielded her from harm. And as the bighearted McKaslin clan and the close-knit Christian community rallied around him, the grief-ravaged drifter felt an awakening in his soul. Could the sweetest blessing of all be standing right before him?

The McKaslin Clan: Ensconced in a quaint mountain town overlooking the vast Montana plains, the McKaslins rejoice in the powerful bonds of faith, family...and forever love.

Don't miss SWEET BLESSINGS
On sale April 2005

Available at your favorite retail outlet.